Dear Uncle Chandler,

Miss Belinda is the bestest nanny in the whole wide world! She takes me out to feed the ducks, helps me take care of my puppy and reads me stories before I go to sleep. And now that she's here I get to play with you too, sometimes. But, Uncle Chandler, who do you have to play with? I bet if you and Miss Belinda got married, you wouldn't be so lonely anymore. Then Miss Belinda would stay here forever. Wouldn't that be fun?

Your nephew,

Steven

Please address questions and book requests to: Silhouette Reader Service
U.S.: 3010 Walden Ave., P.O. Box 1325, Buffalo, NY 14269
Canadian: P.O. Box 609, Fort Erie, Ont. L2A 5X3

VIRGINIA

DIXIE BROWNING

First Things Last

Silhouette Books

Published by Silhouette Books

America's Publisher of Contemporary Romance

SILHOUETTE BOOKS
300 East 42nd St.,
New York, N.Y. 10017

ISBN 0-373-47196-3

FIRST THINGS LAST

This edition published by arrangement with Harlequin Books S.A.

® and TM are trademarks of Harlequin Books S.A., used under license. Trademarks indicated with ® are registered in the United States Patent and Trademark Office, the Canadian Trade Marks Office and in other countries.

Printed in U.S.A.

Dear Reader,

When I learned that *First Things Last* was to be reissued, I thought, oh, my—it was written so long ago it will be terribly politically incorrect by today's standards.

My next thought was, do I care?

Absolutely not. Car models and kitchen appliance colors go out of style. Love never does. Love for a mate, a child, a parent, a friend—love for a pet, or a place. Love is like oxygen; under certain conditions it can cause trouble, but it's impossible to live without it.

So enjoy the story of Chandler and Belinda, and don't worry about whether or not it's in style. I set it in Virginia because I've always had a soft spot for the state. It's beautiful. It's historical. It's also very close to where I grew up, on the Outer Banks of North Carolina. When my family first came to this country in 1620, they landed in Virginia. In Jamestown, to be exact. I went to college in Virginia. Had a ball!

So help me celebrate love and Virginia. They go together like collard greens and cornbread.

Cheers!

Dixie Browning

Chapter One

When the local news came on, Belinda was wrapped into the bound lotus position, her fingers grasping her toes. Her brother, Mickey, was sprawled in the green chair, his eyes alert under lazily lowered lids. Belinda had teased him all their lives about his ability to play possum, and he'd teased her about having a face like a plate-glass window.

"Coffee next commercial?" he drawled.

"You asking or offering?" She released her toes and brought her arms in front of her before unfolding her long, tanned legs.

"You make better coffee."

The teaser flashed across the screen before the commercial came on, and Belinda froze in the process of levering her supple five feet six inches off the floor. Coffee was forgotten as she waited for the commentator to return with the kidnapping story. "Film actress's son reported missing from park," the tag had announced, with a file photo of a familiar face under a cloud of copper-colored hair. Belinda's mind swiftly crossed a span of some six months and several thousand miles to the last time she'd seen that face.

"The five-year-old son of motion picture actress Thalia Faircloth was reportedly kidnapped today from a park near his home. Miss Faircloth, who grew up in Norfolk and still maintains a home here, is in town for the opening of the Shelton Heimann Arts Complex."

No mention of the man who had been with her in Cannes—not that Belinda cared to be reminded of that brief incident. At the time, she had been slightly tight, more than slightly damp, and totally embarrassed.

The news reporter, microphone in hand, continued his crisp delivery. "Miss Faircloth, whose second husband, the younger son of the late C. Morgan Harrington, was killed in a racing pileup in Monaco less than a year ago, was unavailable for comment, but according to her agent, Giles Ebon..."

While the spokesman went on to relate the details of the kidnapping, Belinda was fighting the totally unexpected surge of pain that shot through her at the news that a certain lean, brooding face she had seen only fleetingly six months before was gone. Gone, too, the dark eyes that had swept over her so contemptuously as she perched on one foot, wineglass held high, on the rim of a fountain with the spray slowly drenching her summer cotton dress.

"According to informed sources, there is a possibility that the so-called kidnapping is a hoax. Our eleven o'clock broadcast will carry an update on this story, as well as the details of a new city ordinance. Meanwhile, arson is suspected..."

The voice droned on unheard as Belinda stared blindly at the screen. Six months ago she hadn't even known who Thalia Faircloth was, much less who her husband had been. She'd come across an article about the redheaded actress weeks after her brief glimpse of her, but it had made no mention of the man who had been with her that evening—the man who had so unexpectedly caught Belinda's attention. His dark, Lincolnesque looks, the burning intensity of the gaze that had raked her from bare feet to windblown head, had cut through her like a serrated blade, and she hadn't quite managed to put him out of her mind. After a while, she'd stopped trying.

On that particular evening she had been celebrating with the two older sons of the family for whom she had worked as an au pair all summer. Henri Cadoux had been celebrating his nineteenth birthday. Twenty-two-year-old Georges Cadoux and Belinda, who had been given the evening off in honor of the occasion, were helping him. The three of them had driven from Fréjus up to Cannes to continue the party at an inn with several friends. Both boys had been celebrating since noon, and their high spirits were contagious. When Georges, who had teased Belinda all summer about her yoga regimen, had dared her to prove her sense of balance by holding the stork position on the rim of the fountain outside the inn, she had risen laughingly to the challenge. After all, the tiny, out-of-the-way inn seemed empty except for their own small group. How was she to know that the private room that opened out into the terrace was still occupied?

The wind had picked up, blowing the spray over her, but she had stubbornly refused to concede. She'd held the pose for over two minutes until, drenched and giggling, she had collapsed into Henri's waiting arms. It was at that moment that the couple had emerged and crossed the terrace toward the parking lot. Georges had stared avidly after the woman—had even mentioned her name—but it had been the man, his stern, dark features set in uncompromising lines, who had held Belinda's attention. Their eyes had met and held in the way that sometimes happens between perfect strangers—his, openly contemptuous as they took in her empty wineglass and her boisterous companions. Her own face, unfortunately, was one of those open ones, and she could hardly hope she had managed to hide her fascination.

Odd how she couldn't remember her driver's license number or her social security number, but something like that—a dark, angry-looking face with a pair of laserlike eyes—could cling in her mind like a particularly haunting dream.

And now he was gone. Belinda sat there on the thinly carpeted floor, her knees clutched in her arms as she stared into space. So this was what it was like to lose someone. Good Lord, if learning of the death of a perfect stranger months after the fact could affect her this way, she'd better take herself in hand.

"What d'ya think, huh? Just another publicity

thing?'' Mickey's cynical comment yanked her back to the small two-bedroom apartment.

''Hmm?''

''You're not going to believe this,'' he warned, and Belinda tilted her head up curiously, ''but I've got more than a casual interest in this case.''

She hadn't been *about* to confess the reason for her own interest in the Faircloth case. Of course, Mickey had been referring to the kidnapping and not to the death of the man who had been Thalia Faircloth's husband.

''We've got the case.''

''You've got the *what?*''

''I knew you wouldn't believe me,'' Mickey Massey declared, swinging his lanky frame out of the reclining chair to pace in the confined space. His blond hair, a shade darker than Belinda's sun-streaked crop, looked as if it had been groomed with a twelve-gang harrow. ''The agent called us late yesterday—this fellow Ebon. He told us frankly that he wanted the police in on it, but the Faircloth woman had insisted on calling Dick. Three guesses who insisted on calling the media.'' He stared unseeingly at a toothpaste commercial and then flicked off the set. ''Imagine— old Lovatt actually used to date that redhead sizzler back in high school. And I thought he was slow!''

Dick Lovatt was Mickey's partner in their struggling young detective agency. In his mid-thirties, he looked at least forty, a victim of his own anxious nature. Belinda said, ''Childhood lovers or not, if I'd been in her shoes, I think I'd have gone straight to the biggest and best-known agency in the world. Are you giving me the straight goods, Mickey?" She eyed him suspiciously. Three years her senior, Mickey had been known to play some rather outrageous pranks on her in the past.

"I wouldn't kid about a thing like this, Bel. That's the reason I was home early today; I came directly from the Faircloth condo. It's a mob scene. Disgusting bunch of vultures all but climbing the fences." Ramming his hands into his pants pockets, Mickey Massey frowned at the framed reproduction that had come with the apartment's ghastly furnishings.

It had been all Belinda could do not to toss out the works and start from scratch when she'd first come to stay with her brother three weeks before. But with the agency still struggling to keep its nose above the water and herself unable to find a job to suit her rather obscure qualifications, she had been in no position to make any grandiose gestures.

"So what are you going to do?" Belinda turned toward the closet they called a kitchen to make coffee. "Won't her studio have something to say about her hiring a two-bit outfit run by a couple of comic book detectives?"

"Thanks for the vote of confidence," Mickey said sarcastically. "You know, what bugs me is that it was the agent who got in touch with us. Maybe he had a reason to pick on a small agency. Maybe he wants to get all the PR mileage he can before the thing closes."

"But she can't have just dreamed up the whole thing. Where there's smoke, and all that." Belinda started on a set of sun salutes, her yoga warm-up exercises, while she waited for the coffee to drip.

"Yeah—well, when it's a Hollywood press agent who's sending the smoke signals, you have to wonder. Then, too, it might be a custody fight. This Harrington who was killed in the racing mess—that's a pretty high powered family in these parts. His brother is some big-time architect or something, and Thalia isn't exactly known for her decorous behavior. Curiouser and curiouser," he mused. "I'd be interested in getting a look into the Harrington stronghold."

Belinda missed most of Mickey's conjectures. The news item about the death of the actress's husband had hit her with unexpected force, and no amount of rationalizing seemed to help. Oh, it had been childish, her secret fantasizing—no better than playing with an imaginary playmate. Mickey had teased her unmercifully about her unseen companion back in Richmond, Virginia, where they lived as children. But she was no longer a child. At twenty-five, she should have outgrown such foolishness.

The last of the snow melted in the 60-degree sunshine the next day. It felt more like April than late February. Mickey had fixed his own hasty breakfast and left by the time Belinda got up, as evidenced by the trail of corn flakes across the table. Poor Mickey—the least she could do since she was imposing on his hospitality was to cook him a decent breakfast.

Poor Dick, too. If she could harbor secret fantasies about a man she had seen for no more than a minute, how was he going to handle dealing with a woman half the male population probably was in love with? It was still hard to figure—shy, reticent Dick, the last man on earth anyone would suspect of being a detective, much less of having dated a woman like Thalia Faircloth.

Belinda dressed in a dark-green wool turtleneck and a paisley print skirt. She had bought them both in her junior year at college, and they had given her good service. Examining herself in the mirror, she searched for signs of advanced age, but found none. With characteristic objectivity, she decided she could pass for eighteen as easily as twenty-five—a moderately attractive blonde who tanned lightly at the first breath of spring and remained that way until Thanksgiving. That same heredity provided her with dark, gold-flecked greenish eyes and thick pale hair that never managed to look particularly neat, no matter what she did to it. Her features were nondescript, at best, reflecting her moods with disconcerting accuracy. Excited or happy, she could look almost beautiful, but depressed, she looked decidedly plain. A chameleon, Mickey called her.

Armed with the classified section of the *Virginian-Pilot*, she headed for her first appointment of the day. She had tried three employment agencies with no luck and held out little hope for today's crop. It was past time she launched herself on a career, but with a degree in the creative traditions of folk culture, an interdisciplinary major that included sociology, anthropology, languages, literature and music, she was beginning to despair of her chances. There was a lot to be said for slogging away at something slightly less fascinating. Her three closest friends were already nicely settled as teacher, data processor and dental assistant, and another was actually an Army officer.

At four-thirty, she gave up for the day and headed home. She was either overqualified or totally unqualified, never mind three summers as an au pair and the languages she spoke fluently. Never mind the mini-semester she had spent poking around the hills of West Virginia, loaded down with tape recorder, battery pack, camera and notebooks, capturing the regional music, which had its roots in Elizabethan England, and the narratives that turned everyday events into heroic folk ballads.

The phone rang just as she eased her shoes off and lapsed into a forward bend. Head down, she swore mildly as her hair shed the last of its anchoring pins and slowly uncoiled about her feet. "I'm coming, I'm coming," she snarled, padding over to the littered table.

"Are you home?" Mickey asked her.

"No, I'm aboard the *Calypso* frying channel cats for Jacques Cousteau!"

"Stay there—I'll be there in five minutes!" her brother commanded.

"Sure. I'll toss in another fillet," Belinda muttered sarcastically into the dead instrument in her hand. It had been that sort of day.

She had time to shuck her rumpled clothes and wriggle into a threadbare pair of jeans and one of Mickey's shirts before he let himself in. The excitement that bubbled under his deceptively laconic surface was clearly evident when she flung him a quick glance over her shoulder. "Ham and tomato sandwiches? It's either that or you take me out for a seafood platter."

"Forget food for once, will you? Look, something's developed that's going to put caviar instead of shad roe on our plates."

Belinda went on slicing tomatoes. She had seen her brother's enthusiasm come and go. The agency itself was an enthusiasm that had lasted a lot longer than anyone had expected. "All right, I'll bite, and yes, the pun was intended. What's up?"

After dragging a chair out from under the table, Mickey straddled it and looked at her narrowly from under his straw-colored lashes. His eyes were several shades lighter than Belinda's, but her brows and lashes were darker—an unexpectedly rich chestnut brown. "We know where Thalia's little boy is," he announced dramatically.

"Eureka." Her flattened reception of the news had less to do with her sympathy for the distraught mother than with the guilt feelings that had taken the place of her secret daydreams. "Sorry, Mick. It's super news, really. I guess I'm just tired of wearing my shoes out and taking no for an answer. Maybe I ought to run for a political office. Can't you see me as—"

"Dammit, Bel, shut up, will you? I'm trying to tell you we *know* where Stevie Harrington is! He's with his uncle inside the Harrington estate. At least we're ninety-nine percent certain!"

"So? The child is safe, the mother's delirious with joy, the agent savors the headlines, and Massey and

Lovatt, thanks to her generous token of gratitude, can pay off its hordes of creditors.''

Mickey heaved a sigh, and Belinda turned swiftly and dropped her hands to his shoulders. ''Mickey, I'm being a real witch. I'm sorry for that crack, and I'm delighted the little boy's home again—or soon will be.''

''How delighted?'' her brother asked cautiously.

Shrugging her shoulders under the oversized oxford cloth shirt, she said, ''As delighted as an onlooker can be, I suppose. Do you want it on a scale of one to ten?''

''Do you want a job?''

''Oh, whoa, there!'' She knew Mickey's penchant for trade-offs and she was instinctively wary of this one. ''I'll get a job, don't worry about that.''

''You couldn't get one in Chapel Hill,'' he reminded her with brotherly malice.

''That's a different market altogether! There's no industry to speak of and too many people like me, with unmarketable degrees.''

''You could have stayed with Mom and Dad and looked some more.''

''In a town like Swan Quarter? Jobs there aren't exactly as thick as fleas on a hound dog, you know.'' She'd tried living with her parents, who had moved to the small coastal community in North Carolina after her father had retired from the post office. There was nothing for her there, and she was about to conclude that there was nothing for her in the Tidewater area either.

''I've got a job for you, Bel—on the Harrington

case. Minimum wage, but it'll keep you in junk food until something better comes along.''

She backed away, literally and figuratively. "Oh no, you don't! You're not going to get me mixed up in any of your cops-and-robbers games. I'm not going to repossess any cars or refrigerators for you and I'm *not* staking out some poor woman's husband's girl friend's house.''

At half past midnight, Belinda's curiosity got the best of her. Mickey said, "Look, I promise you, there's nothing to it. This girl I know works at the agency that supplies all the Harringtons' staff. She can cut a few corners about your references.'' Belinda interrupted to declare her references impeccable, and her brother continued as if she hadn't spoken, the light of a dedicated *Rockford Files* fan in his eyes. "After all, I can vouch for you. That's good enough for Maggie—my Soames Agency contact. So all you have to do is be ready to go *if* they need someone to look after the boy. Maggie says the staff is all past retirement age and the housekeeper's an old dragon who runs off every applicant Soames sends out there. We're almost a hundred percent sure the kidnapping's a custody deal, so the Harrington uncle will be doubly cautious. The first thing you have to do is get yourself inside and make sure the kid's actually there. I mean, we'd hate to be sniffing the wrong trail if it's a bona fide ransom deal.''

"*First,* you said. What comes next?'' Belinda asked warily.

"Second, make sure he's not being mistreated. I mean, Thalia might be a little scatterbrained, but that doesn't mean this Harrington dude is any better. After that, it's just a case of finding out the best way to get Steve out again.''

Belinda made one last, exhausted attempt to get out of tackling a job that seemed doomed to failure from the beginning. "Why can't your receptionist do it? After all, this is the sort of thing she was hired for, isn't it?''

"Because Shelvie doesn't know beans about kids, and besides, she looks more like a model than she does a children's nurse.''

"Oh, thanks. I look like a dishmop, I suppose!''

Mickey stood up, raking a hand through his haystack hair. "Look, Bel, it's this simple. Until we know for sure the boy's with his uncle, we can't make a move, and there's no way we can get to the man through ordinary channels. Thalia, poor little thing, is sure Harrington's got him, but that doesn't cut much ice with the authorities, especially when the Harrington name weighs as much as it does in these parts. According to Thalia, it's not the sort of place where a friendly salesman can stroll up to the front door and ask a few pointed questions. We've got to work from the inside. You're a natural for the job because you've had three years of looking after kids. Not only that, nobody will give you a second look once you get past the gate.''

"Thanks,'' Belinda broke in dryly, not sure she appreciated all these comments on her unremarkable appearance.

"And,'' Mickey clinched it, "you need a job.''

It was arranged that *if* Belinda were to be called

for an interview, and if she *were* to get the job of
looking after the Harrington child, she'd make certain
he wasn't being mistreated and then wait for Mickey
to contact her about getting him away. "Look, if they
even call the agency for a baby-sitter," she said with
commendable logic, "it's as good as a confession that
they have him." She gave up in the face of Mickey's
determination.

By the following afternoon, Belinda was practically
chewing her nails. She'd managed to work up a great
deal of righteous indignation on behalf of the unfortunate actress after hearing from Mickey that the
child's despicable uncle had gone so far as to try and
buy the boy from her after Robert Harrington had
been killed. And all because Thalia—she'd almost
come to think of her as "poor Thalia," thanks to
Mickey and Dick—was an actress who had been married once or twice before. As a generously endowed
starlet, she was a box-office hit, if not a critical one,
and thanks to a hustling agent she had come in for
her share of publicity—something the Harrington
family had always actively shunned. And it had not
been all favorable, but then, Mickey explained that
most of the wilder stuff—the drinking and parties—
had been studio hype.

Maggie Douglas, assistant to the manager of the
Soames Agency, called at a quarter to five. Belinda
was expected at the Harringtons' estate in northern
York County the following afternoon at two o'clock.

Struck dumb, Belinda allowed the connection to go
dead before she thought of all the questions she
should have asked. She was out of her mind even to

consider such a harebrained scheme! This was Mickey's problem, not hers. He'd been playing cops and robbers back when he still spoke with a lisp, while Belinda read fairy tales and fantasies and created whole make-believe kingdoms in her imagination. Because she'd been quiet, Mickey had always considered her timid, and the few times she'd kicked over the traces, he'd called her a maverick butterfly.

By noon the next day, Belinda had changed her clothes half a dozen times, redone her hair three times, and lifted the phone more than once to tell her brother it was all off. Only the picture Mickey had brought her of a small boy, his dark, narrow face and enormous black eyes so closely resembling his father's, had kept her from knuckling under to her own lack of confidence.

"I'm a blithering idiot," she muttered to the snapshot of a child feeding a Chinese goose that was almost as large as he was. She knew why she was going to do it, and she wasn't proud of her reasons. All the same, no one needed to know that the night before she had dreamed of a tall, brooding man in evening clothes who had an unforgettable way of marking a woman indelibly with the dark light from his fathomless eyes.

Following the directions given her by Maggie Douglas, Belinda drove up to the large, ornamental gate and stopped. She wasn't fooled by the beauty of the wrought iron and the lush shrubbery. Within minutes a young man, hardly more than a boy, drove up on a quiet motorcycle and opened the gate for her to pass through. He looked harmless enough, but Belinda wondered what would happen if any unauthorized person sought entrance to the Harrington estate. Her imagination had been working overtime since she had agreed to take on this job, and all the James Bond movies she'd ever seen had come back to haunt her.

At least there were no guard dogs in evidence as she drove slowly along the winding, paved driveway. She began to relax a little. This was just a custody battle, after all—unfortunately, a commonplace occurrence these days. She wasn't dealing with the underworld. Not that taking a child from his mother was any minor offense. And then her shoulders began to tense up again as she wondered just how far this Harrington fellow would go to make sure his brother's namesake didn't fall victim to celebrity blight.

The door was opened by an elderly woman who could have been typecast as anyone's grandmother, except for the uniform she wore. Dove gray and quietly fashionable, it was a uniform, nevertheless. This was a dragon?

"You must be Miss Massey from Soames." The woman looked her over warily before opening the door wider. "I'm Martha Duggins, Mr. Harrington's housekeeper. Come in, please. Mr. Harrington's expecting you. I'll take your coat. If you'll come—"

Both women looked upward at a slight sound, and the housekeeper uttered something that sounded almost like a groan. At the top of the broad, curving staircase, a small boy grinned at them over his shoulder as he launched himself down the handrail at the head of the stairs. Instinctively, Belinda moved forward as he picked up speed on the highly polished banister, and she was just in time to catch him as he spun off the down-curved bottom. The impact knocked the breath from her lungs, and she clung to the slight, wiry body with both arms for a moment, staggering to regain her balance. The child was still clasped in her arms when her foot tangled in the edge of a thin, silky Oriental rug and she fell hard on her bottom.

"Oh my lawsey, oh my sakes," the older woman whimpered, bustling around the pair of them and wringing her hands. Gone was her look of wary reserve. To Belinda's amazement, she seemed to have fallen apart at what was really a rather minor accident.

The imp in her lap twisted around to gaze up at Belinda, who returned the look with perfect equanimity. She said, "I'm Belinda Massey. How do you do?"

"I'm Stevie Harrington. How do you do?" he echoed, and then both of them broke into giggles for no good reason at all, unless it was relief that neither of them seemed to have broken anything vital.

"Steven, you could have hurt yourself," the housekeeper accused, still wringing her hands. Belinda realized that she had never actually seen anyone perform that particular act. The term was extremely descriptive. "What's more, your Uncle Chandler told you not to run inside this house."

"I wasn't running, honest!"

"It's the same thing. You can't play indoors like a wild Indian, young man. You'll break something, and like as not, it won't be your own little neck!"

Looking around her, Belinda saw what the other

woman meant. The house was more like a museum than a home, at least from her worm's-eye view, sitting on the floor of the foyer. Of Neo-Georgian styling, its salmon-pink brick exterior was softened by ivy, but the inside was formidable. All the furnishings looked as if they had come over on the second supply ship to Jamestown—the rug that had been her own Waterloo would have been hanging on the wall in any other home.

"Have you come to play with me?" the child inquired. It occurred to Belinda as she lifted him to his feet and arose to her own with balletic grace that she had already accomplished half of her assignment.

At the innocent inquiry, Martha Duggins stopped dithering and bit her lip. The faded blue eyes seemed to be filled with a mixture of hope, embarrassment and frustration. "If you'll just come this way, miss—you didn't hurt yourself, did you? Steven Harrington, you stand right here on this spot and don't you move until I get back, do you hear me?"

Belinda was led from the intimidating foyer past several rather grim-looking portraits and an exquisite boulle breakfront that was very slightly dusty. She pictured the incredibly delicate Venetian bowl filled with a gloriously undisciplined arrangement of flowers, shedding their petals over a lovingly polished surface. Her unquenchable imagination pictured a toy or two and perhaps a leash—better yet, a friendly hound sprawled out on that priceless, if treacherous, oriental rug. *Cool it, Massey. You're not here as an interior decorator!*

They came to a closed door of beautifully paneled

walnut, and the housekeeper tapped softly. "Mr. Chandler? It's the girl from the agency." The relief in her voice was evident.

"The girl from the agency." Belinda wondered if she should have gone around to the service entrance. At least her nervousness seemed to have been lost in the scuffle. Unconsciously, she stretched her spine to its limits, lifting her chin and even her eyebrows in an unconsciously haughty attitude.

"Come in."

The housekeeper's expression took on overtones of sympathy, making Belinda's glossy brown eyebrows lift even higher. The uncle was probably even worse than she had feared, although there had been nothing particularly alarming in the voice—a deep, cultured baritone with only a hint of a drawl.

"Go on inside, miss," the older woman murmured. "I'll look after the boy until you come out."

Now that she was actually there, Belinda could think of all sorts of reasons why she shouldn't be. She'd spent most of the previous night building up a case against the snobbish, heartless man who had stolen the child from his mother for no reason other than that he considered a Harrington, no matter how small, too good to be entrusted to a woman who made her living as an actress.

A portion of her carefully cultivated indignation returned, and bracing herself, she moved boldly forward, her head at an imperious angle.

He was seated behind the desk, silhouetted against a French window, and he stood and waited politely for her to reach him. Not until she was almost at the desk did Belinda get a good look at her prospective employer.

Soft sunlight flowed in to highlight a pair of fathomless eyes, a set of sharply chiseled cheekbones. The room suddenly lurched, and Belinda lifted both hands in an instinctive gesture of rejection. Her mouth opened, but no sound issued forth.

"Miss..." The lean, dark man with the familiar features referred to a paper on the desk before him. "Miss Massey, will you have a seat, please?"

Chapter Two

Miss Massey would. If the chair had not been beside her, she would have ended up on the floor again; the bones in her legs were suddenly weak as rainwater.

"I have here the notes Miss Douglas gave me over the phone, and I assume you've brought along your references." He looked up, his glance narrowing momentarily, and searched her face with those same pitch-black eyes that had impaled her six months earlier. "Miss Massey? Is something wrong?"

Was something wrong? Only that two nights ago the living had died for her, and now the dead had arisen again and none of it was supposed to concern her, anyway!

"Are you feeling all right, Miss Massey? Perhaps I should—"

"No, I'm fine!" The words erupted a little shrilly into the quiet, beeswax-scented atmosphere, and she watched the flicker of curiosity cross his stern features. "Thank you. I—uh—skipped lunch," she improvised hastily.

He shifted slightly in the leather chair, continuing to study her silently while Belinda thought of a thousand reasons for being elsewhere. After an agonizingly long period, the door behind her opened and Chandler Harrington quietly ordered the housekeeper, evidently summoned by a foot-operated buzzer, to provide tea and sandwiches.

Poise was a curious thing. Belinda had seldom been intimidated in her life. She had been interviewed by a countess in a centuries-old castle while she was wearing rubber flip-flops and a fifteen-dollar dress; she had drawn more than a few amused comments by parading her five young charges to the local cinema carrying a gallon thermos of lemonade, a stack of cups and five bags of homemade popcorn, and never turned a hair. She had been called in during one of the countess's luncheons to demonstrate to a group of minor royalty a simple yoga exercise that was supposed to be excellent for skiers.

And she found herself coloring up like an adolescent who'd just committed a terrible gaffe, and all because a would-be employer had ordered tea and sandwiches for her.

"I see you have a bachelor's degree from the University of North Carolina, Miss Massey. I don't think Miss Douglas mentioned your specialty, but I believe you worked for the past three summers with small children in—France, Spain and again in France. Is that right?"

Those third-degree eyes had her babbling out her

qualifications even as one part of her brain cautioned her against revealing precisely where in France she had worked. After all, their one previous encounter would hardly recommend her for the job—and suddenly, she wanted this job very much.

She explained about the degree and her reasons for traveling, living as a part of the family and helping with the children in return for her room and board and a chance to perfect her languages. Hers had been a university-sponsored program, and she'd made some good friends in the various homes in which she had worked.

Martha Duggins brought in a beautifully arranged tray and placed it on the desk between them, leaving as quietly as she had entered. "Help yourself, Miss Massey," Chandler Harrington offered.

Belinda felt as if solid food would choke her, but she nibbled on a thin sandwich of smoked salmon and hard-boiled egg. Her mind was a tangle of confusion. She *wanted* this position! On the other hand, did she want to involve herself in what could turn out to be a messy and highly publicized custody battle? The man was a snob; that was self-evident. He wouldn't allow his small nephew to remain with a woman he considered his social inferior.

It occurred to her that to the Chandler Harringtons of this world, *most* people would be social inferiors—including the daughter of a small-town postmaster, who had so far in no way distinguished herself in life. Heaven help her if he remembered seeing her perched on the edge of a fountain while Georges and Henri stood by with a stopwatch taking bets on how long she could maintain her balance!

Sheer lunacy! What was she thinking of? She'd better be considering what would happen to her if he discovered she was there as a spy for his adversary. If she were smart, she'd set about losing the job before she ever landed it. The boy was obviously being well cared for. His uncle might be an ultraconservative snob of the first order, but he certainly wasn't the sort to neglect a small child. And Mickey couldn't complain about her letting him down if she didn't land the job in the first place.

Nevertheless, when it seemed as if the interview might go against her, she found herself fighting back for all she was worth.

"Miss Massey, your credentials are all in order, but I'm afraid you're just a bit too young for the responsibility. You see, Steve is not an ordinary child."

You're darned right he isn't, Belinda thought angrily. He's the victim of a couple of selfish adults, for starters! Aloud, she said, "I'm twenty-five, Mr. Harrington. Most mothers of children Steven's age are in their twenties."

"Quite right, Miss Massey, but you see, Steve's in the unfortunate position of having a celebrity for a mother and due to his—ah—somewhat unconventional upbringing, he's developed a few behavioral problems."

"So?" Her tone was a distinct challenge, and her eyes held his darker ones determinedly.

"So, Miss Massey, under the circumstances, I think an older woman—"

The door behind her burst open, and a small dynamo erupted into the room. "Uncle Chandler, there's a duck out by the garden house. Can I have him?"

"You must learn not to interrupt when I'm busy, Steve." The words were a firm rebuke, but when he added, "Maybe later on we'll go down to the pond and see if there are any more of them."

Small shoulders slumped, and then the boy turned to Belinda and his eyes lighted up. "Will you catch me again? Are you going to stay here? I have a puppy, only it's too little to leave its mama and I have to wait for it to drink milk out of a bowl."

Grappling with the eager flow of words, Belinda felt her throat tighten at the easy reference to the pup's leaving its mama. Didn't the boy feel anything? Had his uncle told him they were playing a game, or that it was only a short visit?

"Miss Massey won't be staying, Steve. We'll go down to the stables and see the pups on our way to the pond."

That's right, bribe him, Belinda thought furiously. She was glad she wouldn't be around to witness the power play between this wealthy, ruthless man and his unfortunate sister-in-law. The poor child was only a pawn!

Martha Duggins came bustling in, her breathlessness as evident as her flushed face. "Steven, you come back here this minute! I told you not to bother your uncle."

The boy wrapped thin arms around Belinda's knees and buried his face in her lap; her hand went instinctively to brush the incredibly soft hair from his vulnerable nape as her weathervane mind spun around again. It was suddenly imperative that she be allowed to stay.

She heard the housekeeper relating the calamitous events that had occurred on Belinda's arrival, and then Steve was climbing into her lap with the half-shy affection of a child who was never quite sure of his welcome.

Chandler Harrington eyed the tray of sandwiches quizzically, then allowed his eyes to move on to her face, which was rigid with embarrassment by now. If she hadn't known better, she could have sworn she saw a glimmer of amusement there. Staring at him over the child's head, her gold-flecked eyes refused to fall. He murmured something to the effect that he understood now why she had looked slightly shell-shocked at first, and then, somehow, the job was hers.

"Well, that's a blessing, I don't mind telling you," the stout housekeeper muttered. "I'm long past keeping up with the likes of that boy, Harrington or not! If you'll come along, Miss Massey, I'll put you in the room next door to Steve's and you can freshen up."

The housekeeper turned to go, and the child slid to the floor to follow her. Belinda got to her feet and was on the point of going with them when Chandler Harrington spoke again. "Miss Massey will be up in a minute, Martha. Steve, you run along and get your coat and hat. I'll meet you at the side door in a few minutes."

What now? Belinda thought with a sinking feeling. Had he suddenly remembered seeing her before? Had he checked the references she had handed him on her arrival and realized that Fréjus was not far from Cannes, where he had been staying with Thalia Faircloth?

"You did bring a bag, didn't you, Miss Massey? I specified that whomever the agency sent should be prepared to remain. What I failed to tell them I'll tell you now, and you can make up your mind whether you're prepared to undertake the job."

She was standing, half turned to face him. Her head held warily high and her hands still at her sides, she was acutely aware of the stunning magnetism of the man. She could almost feel the heat of his body shimmering across the several feet that separated them.

"Do you have any family, Miss Massey? And if so, what have you told them about your whereabouts?"

"My parents live in North Carolina—Daddy's retired now. They know I'm staying with—in Norfolk, looking for a job. That's all."

"Brothers and sisters?" His level gaze told her nothing, and Belinda bit back the admission of a brother. No doubt he'd want to know all about Mickey, and she was in no position to tell him.

She shook her head, her fingers crossed childishly behind her back. If she were half as transparent as Mickey always accused her of being, the game was up.

The man pursed his rather stern lips consideringly and then, seemingly having come to a conclusion, nodded his head. "You'll be allowed suitable time off, but for the first two weeks, or at least until I tell you otherwise, I'd prefer you didn't leave the premises." He waited for her to object, and when she remained silent he continued. "There will be no visitors, Miss Massey, so if you have a boyfriend, I suggest you get in touch with him immediately and tell him the circumstances of your employment. After a suitable period, of course, these restrictions will be relaxed, but for the time being…"

If it were possible for such a man to look ill at ease, Belinda would have thought that that was behind the lowered eyes, the slight flush that stained those lean, knife-edge cheekbones. He went on. "There's been a certain amount of…dissension in the ranks of the family, Miss Massey. That's as far as I'm prepared to go in the way of an explanation, but if you stay, I'll have to ask for your full cooperation and your undivided loyalty."

"A certain amount of dissension!" The astonishing understatement echoed in her head, arousing a reluctant admiration for the panache of a man who could kidnap his own nephew and then stand there and coolly refer to it as "a certain amount of dissension."

If her feelings about Chandler Harrington had been confused before meeting the man, they were absolute chaos by the time she surveyed the four-poster bed where she'd be sleeping. From the window of the small gray-and-peach-colored sitting room that was part of the lovely suite she'd been given, Belinda looked down on a leafless landscape. Acres of naked pecan trees marched in regimented rows, bordered by the startling yellow fronds of early forsythia. Her eyes followed the meandering figures of Chandler Harrington and his tiny nephew, the boy darting here and there to pick up some small treasure to share with his uncle.

They disappeared into a mellow brick outbuilding whose covering of English ivy enhanced its utilitarian purpose. Belinda turned away, one hand cupping her chin reflectively. This—what did they call it on TV shows?—a caper? A gig? At any rate, this so-called job was turning out to be something quite other than what she'd expected. In the first place, she had come here breathing fire to snatch the poor, helpless victim from the fangs of a pair of wicked dragons. Now, it seemed the dragons were only a harried housekeeper and a fond uncle with a grudge against his beautiful sister-in-law.

Which brought forth another consideration: from what she'd seen in France, the uncle, be he ever so attractive on the surface, had probably been playing around with his brother's wife—or brand-new widow. Either way, it was reprehensible behavior. Belinda had seen with her own eyes the way Thalia Faircloth had been clinging to that strong right arm like moss to the north side of a tree. Thalia Faircloth was no ingenue, and with a virile man like Chandler Harrington—well, it would hardly be a platonic friendship that had them seeking an out-of-the-way inn.

Dinner that night was a strange meal. It was late by her standards, evidently early by Chandler Harrington's. Belinda and Steve sat at one end of the long oval table and their host at the other. Chandler was preoccupied, the child fretful, and Belinda did her best to act as a buffer between them.

"What kind of puppy do you have, Steve?" She unobtrusively cut his chicken for him.

The child fielded the question to his uncle in a whiny voice and was ignored for his troubles. Belinda's mouth tightened, and she turned all her attention to getting the boy through the meal, determined that there wouldn't be a repeat of the occasion while she was there. It would have been unheard-of in the homes where she had worked, having the smaller children staying up to dine with the family. Martha should have known better, even if this glum, brooding man didn't.

By the time she got enough food in the child to hold him until morning, Chandler had spoken exactly five words, and those were dragged out of him by her own stubborn refusal to be ignored.

A routine of sorts was established over the next several days. Belinda found, not entirely to her surprise, that Steve was given to frequent tantrums. While they might have intimidated Martha Duggins, she'd handled far worse, and she anticipated little trouble that she wasn't equipped to deal with. An open child by nature, Steve confided in her freely, revealing a rather pathetic picture of the sort of life he had led in his few short years. Holidays spent with Granny Murdock, whom he didn't like, or with one of several women who had been hired to look after him while his mother was "on location."

Belinda suspected that "on location" might cover a good deal more than mere filming.

"Do you enjoy visiting your uncle Chandler?" she

asked on a morning when they were shelling pecans
for Martha on the promise of a pecan pie for dessert.
The housekeeper had mellowed amazingly now that
she no longer had to worry about keeping up with the
active five-year-old.

"He likes ducks," the child said obscurely, "but
mostly he's too busy to play with me. Mommy says
maybe Uncle Chandler can be my new daddy."

Belinda stored that nugget of information away in
her cluttered mental file. She had seen almost nothing
of Chandler Harrington since the uncomfortable dinner that first night. He was gone during a part of each
day, and the library, which seemed to serve as a sort
of office, stayed securely closed. On one or two oc-
casions, she had heard his voice raised angrily behind
the paneled door.

It was frighteningly easy to forget her reasons for
being there. Martha and her husband, Clarence Duggins, who served as general handyman, seemed con-
tent to putter about at their own speed, leaving Belinda free to structure her time as far as her charge
was concerned. Martha had seemed surprised, but had
readily agreed, when Belinda asked if she and Steve
could have their meals in the roomy, attractive
kitchen, except for dinner, which became an early
supper served in the sitting room of her suite.

If her employer objected, he kept his own council.
Picturing him seated in solitary splendor in the mag-
nificent old dining room, Belinda knew a small
twinge of guilt. He might be an ogre, but he didn't
seem to get much enjoyment from it. He seemed tired,

harried and distracted whenever she happened to catch sight of him.

With his days filled with outdoor activities, Steve was ready for bed by dark. His light meal was followed by a story session or a quiet game, and then a lengthy, relaxed bath before one last story. As a rule, Steve's eyes were closed before she reached the end.

This left long, empty evenings for Belinda to get through with only her uneasy conscience as a companion. The Dugginses had their quarters in a wing off the kitchen, and she had no idea what Chandler Harrington did with his evenings, or if he were even in the house. If she'd thought about it, she might have stuck a few paperback books in her suitcase. She'd read hundreds of them over the summers after her charges were settled for the night. Even though she was supposed to be living as a member of her summer families, it wasn't always convenient for her to join in.

Dressed in her favorite at-home costume, an easy-fitting royal-blue outfit consisting of drawstring pants, a camisole top and a loose, blousy jacket of the same silky cotton fabric, she stretched her arms over her head, placed her bare right foot on the inner surface of her left knee, and stood gazing out the window at the last glimmer of light on the western horizon. Her calf muscles flickered pleasantly as her body automatically balanced itself, and she adjusted her breathing to a slow, steady rhythm. She had promised to show Steve a few of the simpler exercises, but he was seldom still enough.

She wasn't precisely bored. She'd never been bored

in her life. All the same, she had somehow thought, if she had taken time to think at all, that her stay here would be filled with hair-raising escapades, narrow escapes, and spine-tingling intrigue. Instead, her free time had been filled with doubts, confusion over what she was doing there, and nagging curiosity about the man who had haunted the recesses of her mind for the past six months.

She considered making a raid on the library, except for the fact that it also served as Chandler's office. On the other hand, she had a perfect right to go in search of a book, and the library was the logical place to look.

She argued with herself as she wandered restlessly about her room. With all the luxurious appointments of her lovely suite, she thought it odd that she hadn't been allowed a television, or at least a radio. That was carrying an aversion to publicity too far.

Was there any publicity? Was Thalia's agent—Adam or Edam or whatever—getting his mileage out of the "kidnapping"? What a pathetic state of affairs. How could any woman use her own child that way? Or was she as much a victim of the star-making process as her poor baby? Perhaps Chandler was right to try and offer the boy a saner life, but so far, he hadn't shown much promise as a surrogate parent, either. She wondered if maybe she'd better get out before she became too involved with both Harringtons.

Besides, she was growing restless. Trotting through the woods, playing with a litter of retriever pups, and trying frantically to lure migratory geese to within petting distance might exhaust a five-year-old boy, but it left a twenty-five-year-old woman feeling strangely unsatisfied.

The next night she had settled Steve in his bed and was halfway through the bedtime story—it was always the same one; hearing the same words in the same pattern each night seemed to have a comforting effect on the child—when she became aware of another presence in the room. The hair didn't exactly stand up on the back of her neck, but she was aware with every cell in her body that Chandler Harrington had come to stand just inside the door.

Steve's eyes closed with a soft flutter, and Belinda allowed her voice to drone on for a few more minutes before lapsing into silence. She remained seated on the edge of the bed, unable to bring herself to turn and face the man who stood waiting. Without looking over her shoulder, she was sure he hadn't moved a muscle, but she could feel his penetrating gaze on her as she eased the covers up around Steve's thin shoulders and reached over to turn off the light. Only when she could procrastinate no longer did she turn around.

Without a word Chandler turned and led the way, and she followed him through to the sitting room on the other side of her bedroom. In the loose, blue pajamalike outfit, with her hair down about her shoulders, she was uncomfortably aware that she looked scarcely old enough for the position she held, and the knowledge rankled. Chandler Harrington was intimidating enough without that. Tonight he wore a flawlessly cut three-piece suit of some dark material that emphasized the differences in their ages and positions. Belinda was far more accustomed to jeans and sneakers. She glanced down at her bare feet, wishing she at least had the dignity of shoes.

"How are you getting along with my nephew, Miss Massey?"

She had forgotten the physiological effect of that voice, which sounded like chocolate-coated steel. "Just fine," she muttered, avoiding the eyes that could compound the paralyzing effect.

"I get the impression that he looks on you more as a contemporary."

"I hope not!" Her head came up at the remark, and she examined his face for censure, but found none. "I think I'm perfectly capable of handling a child firmly without endangering our friendship."

He moved about the room restlessly, picking up first one small accessory and then another and replacing each without a glance. Belinda waited for what was to come next. He wasn't the sort of man who stopped by just to pass the time of day with an employee. In fact, now that she studied him more closely, he looked as if he hadn't slept at all since their initial interview. Beneath his chisled cheekbones, the hollows were gaunt, the grooves in them deeper than ever, and his eyes showed evidence of too many late nights.

All of these things should have made him look terrible, but instead he was even more magnetically attractive than ever. Belinda felt an overwhelming need to touch the thick, raven-dark hair, to press away the furrows in his high forehead, to comfort him as she had comforted his nephew earlier in the day when he had tripped on a root in the pecan grove and gone sprawling.

"I wasn't questioning your ability, Miss Massey." He said quietly and then impatiently, "I can't go on calling you Miss Massey! You're practically young enough to be my daughter." His stern mouth twisted in a smile that was all the more effective for its rarity, and Belinda felt as if the sun had suddenly changed course and risen again.

"Call me Belinda then, Mr. Harrington. And I doubt that you're as old as my father. I was a late blessing—an afterthought. He's sixty-nine."

"At the moment, I feel like a hundred and sixty-nine. Look, would you care for coffee or a drink? I need something to keep me going for the next few hours." Astoundingly, his eyes seemed almost to be pleading with her, and she nodded with the fatalistic resignation of someone who had just jumped off a bridge, knowing there was no way to go but down.

The housekeeper was panting when she brought in the tray into the sitting room, and Belinda regretted not having offered to fetch it herself. She settled into a wide brocade wing chair and tucked her feet out of sight. She'd seen Chandler's eyes on them more than once, and it made her feel oddly vulnerable.

They talked desultorily about the weather, and about the eclectic collection of treasures brought home by several generations of seagoing Harringtons and displayed throughout the house. She wanted to ask him why he hadn't followed in their footsteps, but before she could frame the question, his quick, restless mind had shifted again to his nephew.

"I'd planned to spend more time with the boy, but somehow, with the best intentions in the world, I find myself booked into too many appointments that can't be postponed, too many things that can't be delegated..."

Belinda's unruly mind interjected, *And too many dinner dates you don't want to miss.* She studied his averted face wistfully as he leaned back against the cushions of the love seat, his long legs extended before him and crossed at the ankle, momentarily allowing his tiredness to show. "Duggins doesn't seem to get around to trimming dead branches from those trees. Test them before you climb too high," he said absently, as if his mind were already on more pressing matters.

So he had been watching them prancing around the yard, jumping, climbing and swinging like a couple of monkeys. The knowledge brought a tightening to her stomach muscles. The childish exertion had helped to drown out her nagging conscience and seemed to have a definite calming effect on Steve. His tantrums had diminished noticeably, although his sleep was still troubled.

"I'll direct him to the small oak," she murmured, uncomfortably aware of the way Chandler's gaze had intensified as it moved over her.

Was he suspicious? Had he discovered her connection with Mickey or Thalia? Or was he merely exercising the prerogative of any healthy male in the company of a reasonably attractive female? The thought had her fingers nervously making tiny pleats in the hem of her camisole.

"Do you like caring for children, Belinda?"

That was an easy one. She explained about the mother's helper system that had enabled her to travel at a fraction of the usual cost. "It's great for polishing up on your accent, but in the real world, there's not all that much demand for employees who speak three languages, can't spell in any of them, type about three words a minute, and play the hammer dulcimer and the penny whistle passably well."

That led to a discussion of some of her experiences in attending folk festivals and traveling through the West Virginia mountains and foothills in search of indigenous music. It was a far safer topic than her travels abroad. By the time Chandler stood to go, he had learned far more about her than she intended, and she knew no more about him than she had in the beginning.

He lifted his shoulders tiredly. It was almost a stretch, but not quite, and she saw that some of the grayness had left his face. He looked considerably more relaxed than he had at first, and the knowledge brought her a small surge of pleasure.

Tightening her lips, she stared fixedly at a Staffordshire bowl on the coffee table. *None of that, Belinda, my girl!* If there was one thing she could not afford, it was to allow her sympathies to swerve from the victim—or the victim's mother—to the kidnapper. Uncle or not, this man had actually stolen a child from his mother, and she was there to help see that justice was done!

Correction—she was there because she'd caught the gaze of a stranger on a summer evening six months before and had been haunted by him ever since, she reminded herself resignedly. And because her brother had a knack of twisting her around his conniving little finger!

Chandler strolled over to gaze out her window— the same window she had looked down from that first afternoon to see him wandering through the bare, sprawling pecan trees, a small boy clinging trustingly to his large hand.

"Oh, by the way, there was a call for you earlier, Belinda."

Her eyes flew to his face, and she tried unsuccessfully to read the expression there. It had to have been Mickey; no one else knew where she was.

"The boyfriend, I assume. Didn't you explain to him that you'd be out of touch for a few days?"

"What did he want?" Belinda asked cautiously, avoiding a direct reply. She'd uncoiled from the chair and now was poised warily, half expecting to be exposed and sent on her way in the next breath.

Chandler's gaze hadn't moved from her, and she wondered if the guilt she felt were scrawled across her face. But it wasn't her face that held his attention. His darkly shadowed lids had lowered as his eyes followed the half-hidden contours of her body; she could feel them moving over her breasts as palpably as if the jacket and camisole weren't even there.

As if snatching back his wandering attention, Chandler said, "I told him you'd call him back. You may use the phone in the library."

Her breath was expelled in a sigh of relief. She definitely wasn't cut out for this *Perils of Pauline* kind of thing—not when she had an unquenchable hankering for the villain. "Thank you." Uncertain whether he meant for her to return the call now or not, she waited for him to make a move.

Again she was treated to that devastatingly attractive smile. Slow, almost reluctant, it warmed his eyes like newly fanned coals. "As for what he wants from you, I could hazard a guess. He's a lucky young man, Belinda."

If he had suddenly lapsed into a soft-shoe routine, she couldn't have been more shocked! In spite of all she knew—or at least strongly suspected—about Chandler Harrington's relationship with women, including his own sister-in-law, it came as a shock to hear him make a remark of that sort. Though heaven knows why it should have, she admitted reluctantly. He might be a conservative, pillar-of-society type, but he was certainly no monk, not when he fairly radiated virility even when he was obviously dog tired.

She didn't know whether to thank him or put him in his place for making unnecessarily personal remarks. It occurred to her that she was overreacting to what was only a casual compliment, after all, and she stalked across to her bedroom to find a pair of shoes. "I'll be down in a few minutes, then, if you don't mind." Her voice was little more than a muffled growl, but he nodded and let himself out with only a mild rebuke.

"I wouldn't have bothered to come tell you about the call, Belinda, if I'd minded."

Chapter Three

Belinda halfway expected Chandler to be waiting to monitor her call, but the library seemed to be empty when she hurried downstairs. Her feet in the thin chamois exercise sandals made no sound on the antique oriental rug.

"Mickey? Are you insane?" He had answered on the first ring, as if he'd been sitting by the phone.

"What the devil's going on there, Bel? I thought you were going to get in touch with me?"

"Don't be silly! You told me to wait until—until I decided whether or not I wanted to stay," she said cautiously.

Falling into a lifelong pattern, they argued without any real animosity until Mickey insisted that she meet him somewhere in the area the following night. "Mickey, I can't do that! Mr. Harrington specifically told me I was to stay on the premises and contact no one until he gave me permission." She was anxious to finish the call and be done with it. There was no way her employer could know, even if he overheard her end, that Mickey was her brother, much less that he was a detective hired to recover Steve Harrington.

"Look, we can't talk now over the phone. You've got to meet me. If you can't leave, then get me in there somehow. Are there any guard dogs? What sort of security system does Harrington have?"

The whole game was beginning to pall. "Oh, Mickey, for Lord's sake, the only dog I've seen around here is a golden retriever, and she's too busy with her litter to be worrying about the likes of you. I'll meet you at the main gate, but just for a minute. In fact, I may just leave with you!" she declared rashly, forgetting the possible need for caution. "I'm not cut out for this sort of business."

She knew she wouldn't, though. She knew she was going to stick as close to Chandler as she possibly could, regardless of who was right and who was wrong in the matter of Stevie Harrington.

"And if that's the act of a sane, mature woman, then I'm a three-toed sloth," she muttered, hanging up the phone with an impatient oath.

The library, with its floor-to-ceiling books and several tall French windows opening out onto a flagstone patio, was lighted only by a floor lamp behind the desk. Changing course abruptly on her way out, Belinda decided that now was as good a time as any to stock up on reading matter for the empty evenings to come. As welcome as that night's tantalizingly brief interlude had been, it would hardly be repeated. In fact, she thought, Chandler must already have gone out for the night. He hadn't exactly been dressed for a quiet evening at home alone.

Browsing through a large collection of technical books on shipbuilding, she found a section of modern novels that leaned heavily toward sea stories. Her father had been in the Navy, and she had been weaned on C. S. Forester and others of his ilk until she had discovered mythology. From then on, she had followed her own drummer.

Smiling in recognition, she plucked out a copy of Frank Herbert's *The Dragon in the Sea,* a science-fiction novel she'd read some years back. She had always been fascinated by the inventiveness of the genre. She took that and a copy of *Run Silent, Run Deep,* deliberated on whether or not to turn off the light, and shrugging, left it on as she closed the door quietly behind her.

Settling herself on the love seat in her sitting room, she opened the Herbert book. Odd to think that she and Chandler shared a fondness for both science-fiction and sea stories—or maybe not too odd, at that. Millions of people read both categories. Snorting derisively, she admitted to herself that she was simply reaching for a bond of some sort.

The familiar words blurred as her mind wandered out through the wrought-iron gates and beyond. Where had he gone tonight? Who was he with right this minute? Certainly not Thalia—not when they were at daggers drawn over the child sleeping in the next room. Was that the reason he'd looked so wretched? His conscience was probably giving him the very devil. He wasn't a man who bent the bonds of his own integrity easily—that much she knew instinctively, no matter how things looked on the surface.

For that matter, why had he taken the child in the first place, knowing full well Thalia would know whom to blame? And what did he hope to gain? Did he honestly mean to take his sister-in-law to court and prove her an unfit mother? Or was he just trying to scare her into staying home and looking after her child instead of trusting him to a series of baby-sitters while she ran around filming and partying all over the world?

And what made Chandler think he was so great an influence for a small boy? Since that first day, he'd hardly had time to pat him on the head in passing. A child needed at least one constant source of love in his life, and at the moment, it looked as if Stevie was on his own.

Belinda brooded for a while, the book forgotten. Soon her eyes closed and her hand fell away from page five of *The Dragon*. The book slid to the floor with a quiet thud.

Sometime during the night she opened her eyes and frowned at the glare of the table lamp as she waited for the sound that had awakened her to be repeated. She felt stiff and thick-headed, not to mention chilled to the bone. She hadn't intended to fall asleep on the love seat.

A shutter banged noisily, and she heard the soft branches of the wisteria scraping against the window. Fighting her own inertia, she got stiffly to her feet and padded across to the sitting room to see if the noise was coming from one of her shutters.

The proverbial watched pot! Belinda almost went to sleep on her feet as she stood there, huddled against the chilliness, waiting for the noise to come again. She was unusually aware of the normal night sounds of the old house—the creaking of cooling heat ducts, the loud ticking of a clock.

It was late. The wind had picked up considerably, and it was black as pitch outside—squally feeling, like a spring thunderstorm. She decided she may as well go to bed, since the stubborn shutter refused to bang while she watched, and anyway, there were dozens of windows in the house. It could have been any one of them.

Shrugging out of her wrinkled jacket, she allowed the straps of the camisole to slide from her shoulders and felt for the drawstring of her pants. Half tempted to fall into bed as she was, she shored up her sleepy determination and stumbled to the bathroom to brush her teeth and splash water over her face. She'd scrub it thoroughly tomorrow; thank goodness she seldom bothered with makeup unless she were going out somewhere.

She was brushing her hair when the shutter banged again. The sound had definitely come from her sitting room. At the same time she heard Steve's drowsy voice, mumbling something unintelligible. The problems that had developed over a period of years couldn't all be quickly resolved. He still occasionally flew into a short, stormy tantrum, and more than once she had heard him talking in his sleep.

Dropping her brush on the dresser, she hurried to the sitting room to see if she could hook the shutter closed until something could be done about it in the morning. She was struggling to open the sticking window when the door opened behind her and Chandler came in.

"You might have knocked," she rebuked him, straining against the sticking window.

"I thought you'd be asleep. Move over and let me do it."

Stung by his calm assumption of superiority, she strained harder. "I can do it," she grunted, bracing her feet to gain leverage. She struck the top of the frame with the heel of her hand, abrading her skin painfully, and then shoved at the stubborn double-hung window as the shutter banged mockingly in her face. The light was still on in the room, and she was acutely aware of the looming figure beside her, even though she refused to glance at him. Pushing at the immovable object, she wished she had gone in for pumping iron instead of yoga. The philosophy and discipline were all very well, but when a window needed opening, or a jar lid loosening, she was out of luck. At the moment, she'd have traded a whole bushel of tranquility for a pound or two of muscle!

Warm, hard hands closed over her bare shoulders and moved her firmly aside. She glared up into Chandler's imperturbable face, and then he calmly reached up and unlatched the window before raising it easily. She could have hit him! "I suspect the hook rusted out. I'll mention it to Duggins in the morning. Meanwhile, I hope you're not claustrophobic. You'll have to put up with having it closed.''

Securing the inner fastenings, he closed the half-shuttered window again and turned to smile at her in a manner she interpreted as condescending. ''Feels like spring, doesn't it? Wind's swung around to the south-east.''

''I could have done it,'' she snapped, irritated by his bland demonstration of superiority. He wore a navy-blue silk bathrobe over matching pajama pants, and she could see from the loosely tied sash that he disdained the wearing of a top. Every nerve in her body was painfully aware of the intimacy of the situation, and she was horribly afraid he'd see just how strongly she was affected by his nearness. Good Lord, how could she convince him she was a mature, level-headed woman, perfectly capable of taking on the responsibility of looking after his nephew, when she reacted to his presence like a starving man at a banquet?

''Did the boy wake up?'' he asked, taking a firm grip on her elbow and leading her across to the love seat.

She dropped to the comfortable velvet seat readily enough, quelling the quick surge of disappointment when he took the nearby chair. ''Not really. He whimpered and then mumbled a little, but I don't think he woke up.''

''Is he having trouble at night?'' His eyes had moved from her face, still flushed from earlier exertions, to her bare shoulders, and she was uncomfortably conscious of the fact that she was still wearing a skimpy camisole top, the drawstring pants, and little else—and the thin, silky cotton was even more revealing than her utilitarian pajamas.

"Sometimes he talks," she murmured distractedly, "but he doesn't usually wake up. At least, he hasn't since I've been here." Suddenly, the past few days seemed like half a lifetime. She reminded herself forcefully that she didn't *know* this man, had never seen him before she had come there, so why this unsettling feeling of déjà vu? Was it only because she had noticed a distinguished-looking man with a particularly intense gaze one night in Cannes? Good Lord, she was a healthy, normal woman! She noticed any attractive man, just as she was aware of having been noticed herself. It was all part of the game—only this man, with no more to recommend him than a lean, bony face and a brooding, slightly sardonic gaze, had crept into the hidden recesses of her mind and become a part of her very consciousness.

"You like the boy, don't you? I've watched you with him. You're...very caring. Natural, unselfconscious, and yet you're always in control. It's what he needs, Belinda. I'm glad I found you."

The flattering assessment of her relationship with her charge left her feeling guilty as well as hopelessly vulnerable. She found her eyes straying everywhere except to his face—to his beautifully shaped hands, with their dusting of black, wiry hair and the sensitive, neatly trimmed nails; to his lean, muscular thighs under the thin sheath of silk, where his robe had fallen open.

Stop it, Belinda! You're asking for trouble. She

managed to tear her gaze away from her employer long enough to glance meaningfully at the small ormolu clock.

"Yes, I know—it's late," he dismissed. "Belinda, I deplore any sort of dishonesty. I think it's time I leveled with you." The words shook her badly, and she stared at his half-averted face. Steepling his fingers, he continued to regard them as he said, "I don't know how much you know about Steve. The news—I had hoped the media wouldn't get hold of it, but then, that's part of the reason for all this, I guess." He shrugged, still avoiding her eyes, and she couldn't have answered if her life had depended on it.

"Steve's father was my younger brother. He was killed in a racing pileup last summer. Before that, the boy spent a great deal of time with his maternal grandmother. The term *maternal* is ironic, in her case." His lips twisted bitterly. "Unfortunately, I wasn't always available when he needed a place. His mother is Thalia—you might have heard of her—Thalia Faircloth. She was a Murdock, from Suffolk, before she became an actress. At any rate, she—ah—"

He hesitated, as if seeking the most diplomatic way of describing Thalia and her career, as well as his own relationship to her. But, of course, he wouldn't go that far, she reminded herself. After all, he was only explaining the child's problems, not his own.

"Let's just say that the boy hasn't had the best—most attentive care since his father died. Actually, there were problems before that. The—ah—marriage wasn't a particularly successful one." Once more he seemed embarrassed, and Belinda wondered if he

were trying to shift the blame for his own part in
wrecking his brother's marriage. Still, it wasn't her
job to judge, much less to condemn on what was, at
best, circumstantial evidence. All the same, she
wished it had been otherwise. It hurt like the devil to
think that this incredibly attractive man had some
very human weaknesses.

He looked up as if expecting a comment of some
sort, and their eyes met and clung in a way that shook
Belinda to the core. A shadow flickered across Chandler's face, and then he seemed deliberately to shake
himself out of his oddly distracted mood. "But you're
not interested in all this ancient history. I only thought
it might help you in dealing with the boy. Martha
can't begin to handle him, and unfortunately, I can't
always be here to take over." He stood up and
crossed restlessly to the half-shuttered window.
"There are circumstances bearing on this situation
that I can't go into now, but do what you can to make
him feel more secure, will you? For one reason and
another, he's had a tough row to hoe. I plan to do
everything in my power to see that he has a decent
chance."

Her every instinct cried out to tell him exactly who
she was and why she was there. As bad as things had
been before, his confidence in her only made her own
position more invidious. Oh, why couldn't Mickey
solve his own problems and leave her out of them?
Why couldn't Chandler and his sister-in-law reconcile
their differences for the sake of the child? If that
meant marrying after a suitable period, so be it. The
half-truths, the bits and pieces of this troubled triangle

were no concern of hers. Once she was out of there, she'd get as far away as possible, so that there would be no reminders of a pair of intensely thrilling dark eyes and a slow, rare smile that could twist her heart without even trying!

They both heard it at once. Chandler moved silently across the room, and Belinda came to her feet in a single lithe movement to join him in the door of Steve's bedroom. The child whimpered. Tiny sobs, as if he were winded, shook his thin little body, and Belinda moved instinctively to go to him. She was caught and held by Chandler's firm grip on her arm, pulled back against his hard body. "Wait," he breathed against her ear. His voice stirred tendrils of hair and raised goose bumps along her spine. She could smell the faint aroma of his sandalwood soap. "He's only dreaming. He'll have forgotten by morning. If we wake him now, he'll only have to deal with it."

Lifting her mouth to within an inch of his ear, she whispered urgently, "Maybe he should. He has to deal with whatever's troubling him sooner or later."

One arm around her waist, Chandler pulled her back through the dressing room that separated the two bedrooms. His voice was still lowered, a husky rumble as he said, "But not now. Not when there's no way I can reassure him about the future. A week—a month, at best, and maybe I can come up with a solution."

Her heart lurched painfully at the thought of what that solution would be. So much for her decision to clear out and leave it all behind her. As illogical as it was, she had an idea that she'd be a long time shedding the spell this man had unknowingly cast over her. She knew both more and less than she needed to to deal intelligently with the situation, and in spite of all reason, that situation was growing more and more complex as she was forced to come to terms with the powerful attraction Chandler held for her.

There was an endless day to be gotten through. Belinda made puddles of milk in her oatmeal as she relived the unlikely episode in the hours before dawn. It had been almost four o'clock when Chandler had left her, and he had done so with a long, intimate look that had shaken her thoroughly. It was as if he, too, found himself catching glimpses of some nebulous affinity, some deep-seated magnetism that throbbed beneath the mundane surface of their relationship.

Not that the surface was all that mundane, she quickly reminded herself. She was there under false pretences, and for the life of her, she didn't know what was in the best interests of the child. Without quite knowing how it had come about, she seemed to be in the position of judge.

The morning was spent in the kitchen with Martha, who allowed Steve to help her bake a cake. Belinda snapped beans and listened as the child prattled on at ninety miles an hour. Martha murmured an occasional response as she deftly added the ingredients to the old-fashioned 1-2-3-4 cake, while Belinda examined Chandler's words for a clue of how best to deal with his problems.

The fitful rain ended about eleven, and with the

cake enveloping the whole kitchen wing of the house in a delicious buttery, vanilla-y aroma, Belinda dashed away to get Steve's and her coats for a run around the grounds before lunch. Steve's appetite was poor enough as it was, and after scraping out the batter bowl, it would take an hour of outdoor exercise to put an edge on it again.

She was passing the library door when she heard Chandler's angry voice on the phone. Her steps slowed instinctively, and with no thought of eavesdropping, she heard him telling someone that he knew precisely how much their promises were worth, and that no, he would not reconsider. And then he said quite clearly, "All right, Thalia, I'll meet you for dinner, but on my terms."

The sound of the phone crashing into the cradle was clearly audible where she stood, rooted guiltily to the spot, and only when she heard Chandler's firm tread coming toward the door did she move again. She was on the second stair when the door opened and she found herself helplessly riveted by his angry glare.

Even as she watched, the anger faded, to be replaced by a sort of weary resignation. "Are you and the boy managing to keep occupied?"

"He—we—Martha's baking a cake. Steve's been helping her." She couldn't seem to detach her eyes from his, and the tension was agonizing. "I—I thought I'd take him for a run outside now that the rain's stopped. I heard a flock of geese a while ago and I thought…" She allowed her voice to dwindle away as she finally managed to recover her gaze. Hurrying up the stairs, she had almost reached the top when he called after her.

"I'll go with you. I could do with a breath of fresh air myself."

Steve, thrilled at the unexpected bonus of his uncle's company, made quick little forays to investigate a bird's nest and a tiny chipmunk burrow that he was sure must lead to an underground cavern. Chandler and Belinda strolled along after him, both seemingly lost in private thoughts. Belinda's concerned the piece of a conversation she had overheard: So Thalia and Chandler were in communication. That made her position there even more of a farce—not that it had ever been anything else, she thought hopelessly.

Her mind wandered along a wistful channel; what if, instead of beating the bushes for some nonexistent job that suited her peculiar talents, she had gone to the Soames Agency in the first place and applied for a job along the lines of those she had held in Europe? That would have been reasonable enough. Just because she didn't intend to make a life's career of tending other people's children didn't mean it wouldn't do in a pinch. And what if the call from Chandler had come through and they had sent her along and she had got the job on the up and up? Then she'd have nothing to hide from a man who professed to despise dishonesty of any sort. They'd be starting even, with no hidden handicaps.

Kicking out in frustration at a fallen branch, she reminded herself of the two handicaps that refused to go away. In the first place, Chandler wouldn't have needed her services except that he had more or less kidnapped his own nephew, and in the second place, she might not have considered the job at all except for a fleeting contact with a man she found it impossible to forget! So much for the *what ifs.*

"Penny for them?" Chandler murmured. He was dressed more casually than usual in dark corduroys, a soft chamois shirt and a well-worn jacket of olive drab.

Belinda regarded him with wary interest as he bent to pick up a small pebble and send it flying to knock a cluster of nuts from one of the trees. "Lucky shot," she taunted, glad of a diversion from the relentless pursuit of her worrisome thoughts.

"Would you care to make a small wager?"

Entering into the spirit, she pointed to a hollow in an ancient cypress near the pond. "I'll land three out of five shots in the hole or pay a forfeit," she declared, trusting her one season as a bench warmer in the neighborhood Little League would stand her in good stead.

"You're on. Stevie, help me gather some ammunition." After scampering across the rather unkempt grounds to the more formal gardens near the house, the eager child came back with pockets filled with small river rocks.

The game brought a gleam of determination to Belinda's gold-shot eyes, as well as a flush of color to her cheeks. The look of taunting triumph Chandler sent her when her second pebble fell short swiftly changed into something less easily definable. Flustered at recognizing an element of admiration in it, she hastily tried a third shot that came nowhere near

the target tree, and Steve crowed his support of the
"men's team."

"I'll *men's team* you, you rascal!" she cried, chasing him until they both fell laughing on the damp, leaf-plastered ground. "Just for that, I'll eat your cake and mine, too, after lunch." They tumbled laughingly on the ground, with Belinda taking care not to allow the boy's clothes to come in contact with the sodden earth, until Chandler insisted they witness his two winning shots.

After that, they sauntered down to the pond, gazing out at the half-dozen or so migratory wildfowl that had come to rest there. Steve was beside himself, calling out to lure them closer. Chandler mimicked the Canadian geese with a plaintive honking sound, and Belinda doubled up with laughter when the regal gander cast a disdainful look his way.

"Son, why don't you go find Duggins and ask him for a few ears of feed corn. He has a bag of it in the garden shed."

The boy was off like a shot, his thin little legs in the corduroy jeans leaping over the fallen pecan branches that littered the grove. Both adults gazed after him with unsmiling compassion. "Something has to be done, and soon," Chandler murmured.

Wheeling away instinctively, Belinda sought out an ancient wooden bench, considered the mossy, leaf-littered surface, and decided against risking it. The thing looked as if it had been there since the Jamestown expedition. She had enough on her mind just now without having to contend with a broken bone, or at least badly injured dignity.

Chandler took off his jacket and spread it on the ground in the lea of a thick hedge of Russian olive. "At the rate poor old Duggins gets around these days, we might as well be prepared to wait," he observed dryly, gesturing for her to be seated.

"What happened to the boy on a motorcycle who let me in the first day I was here?" she asked idly. The fact that she would be seeing Mickey again made her think of her arrival there such a short time before. She had been frightened, confused and reluctant then. She was no longer frightened. Reluctant? She wasn't sure. But confused? More than ever! By the boy, the man, and, most of all, by her own irrational longings. Chandler's answer broke into her thoughts.

"Pete? Oh, he works part-time, goes to school part-time. Until I moved back here several months ago, the Dugginses, Pete, and an occasional cleaning woman took care of the place. According to Martha, though, it gets harder and harder to find trustworthy help these days."

What could she say to that? Sitting, knees drawn up and clasped with her arms, on one side of the open jacket, she stared fixedly at one of the drab female geese. The small flock was swimming gracefully along the far bank.

"Belinda?"

Caught off guard by something in his voice—a tentative, questioning note—she turned, and then wished she hadn't. He was too close. He had joined her on the jacket, sitting as she was, facing the pond. A cool sun shone from a pale, yellow-gray sky, revealing a fine network of lines at the corners of his eyes.

"Belinda, you've already made a big difference around here. Have I thanked you for all you're doing for Steve?"

Tearing her eyes away, she stared at her knees in the watch plaid trousers. "That's only what I was hired for."

"It's more than that. I'd almost forgotten how pleasant it was to hear laughter around the house, to see flowers in vases and a bowl of nuts on the hearth. I find I enjoy a certain amount of...untidiness."

When she didn't respond, he spoke again. "Belinda?" His hand came down on her knee, and she stared at it as if she had never seen a hand before. *Don't be nice to me,* she pleaded inwardly. *Don't make me feel any worse than I already do!* "Belinda, why, at your age, aren't you married and making a home for a husband and children of your own?"

Grasping at any excuse to avoid the dangerous entrapment, she replied brittly, "You're a little behind the times, Mr. Harrington. These days, a woman doesn't have to settle for diapers and dishwashing. She can choose to be or do anything at all now. Maybe I'd prefer being a lawyer, a doctor, or maybe even an—an airline pilot," she invented boldly.

His hand was still on her knee and he shook it, dislodging her clasped arms. "Oh, so that's why you took all those fanciful courses. So you could be an airline pilot?" he taunted playfully.

"I could have been thinking about a career in the diplomatic service."

"Were you?"

She wished he'd move his hand. Without seeming

painfully coy, she couldn't, and his touch was burning right through the thin flannel of her slacks. "Hardly," she shrugged. "Maybe I'm just a case of arrested development. I took what I wanted from school, and it was only a fluke that they let me take a degree. The folk movement was still big then, and I just happened to mix in the right ingredients to come up with an acceptable recipe."

"This instrument you play—tell me about it. I'm not sure I even know what it is." His hand had finally dropped from her knee, but now it was dangerously close to her own, with one finger making daring little excursions to brush against the slender bones of her wrist.

"Actually, I play several, but none particularly well. Mama insisted that I take piano lessons from the first grade on through high school, and after that it was easy enough to pick up a smattering of guitar, banjo, mandolin. I tried the fiddle, too, but my roommate at the time threatened to butter my bow. I can play a few recognizable tunes on the penny whistle and the recorder, but my favorite is the dulcimer."

"I'd like to hear you sometime."

She turned to laugh at him and was disconcerted to find his face too close to her own. "No, you wouldn't," she managed with a slightly unsteady voice. "It's strictly an acquired taste."

"I can think of another taste I'd like to acquire," he murmured deeply, and then it was too late. Like a light-blinded rabbit, she sat there as his face moved the few inches it took to meet hers. Their lips met—just barely—and clung. He was not touching her except for the finger that had hooked over her own, and the warm, firm lips that moved against hers with incredible sensitivity.

Stunned by the dichotomy of her senses, she allowed the kiss to go on and on. One part of her was aware only of Chandler—of the scent of his chamois shirt, of the sandalwood soap he favored, and the exciting masculine essense of his healthy body, the taste and the texture of his warm, sensitive mouth as it moved with incredible gentleness over hers. Another part of her consciousness was aware of every single thing that went to make up the time-out-of-time movement—the penetrating coldness of the ground, the faint warmth of the early March sunshine, the smell of wet earth and pond life, and the spicy aroma of the cedars and cypress trees that rimmed the dark water.

From the distance, Stevie's war whoops came to her ears. She was almost glad, in a way. Demanding absolutely nothing of her, Chandler had managed to coerce the heart and soul from her. If it had gone on much longer, he could have had her body, as well.

Chapter Four

As the sun gave in to the handful of ragged clouds and resigned itself to a pale, watery reign, the day began to go awry. The geese failed to succumb to Steve's ardent pursuit, and Chandler became more and more distracted. By the time they assembled for lunch, he was positively morose.

To top it off, Steve's behavior was worse than usual. He picked at his food and whined when Belinda tried to lead him away for a nap, crying out angrily that his mother never made him take an afternoon nap. Belinda found her own patience in short supply, and not until she had held the child, kicking and screaming, and rocked him until he collapsed in a hot little bundle of sleepy tears did she give herself over to worrying about the meeting with Mickey.

Moving with a slow, soothing rhythm in the old Boston rocker, she hummed monotonously, her arms curving around their burden as she allowed her thoughts full range for a few moments. Then, not caring for the direction they took, she jerked her attention back to the child, staring down at his flushed face, the dark hair that fell across his high forehead in a way that brought a painful lump to her throat. He was so *much* like his uncle.

It wasn't fair to Steve for her to remain there. Poor darling, he soaked up affection like a sponge, and his very need seemed to stimulate her supply of love—and not all of it maternally directed toward him, she was sadly afraid.

Rising carefully, she crossed to the twin bed and lowered the sleeping boy, pulling a spread over his slightly undersized body. She laid a hand on his cheek and frowned fleetingly at the warmth of his skin. From experience she had learned that children could run a temperature from the slightest of causes. His temper tantrum could have brought it about, but he'd bear watching, all the same.

While Steve slept, Belinda showered and shampooed her long, sun-streaked hair. Darker now that it was winter, the ends still bore traces of the previous few summers on the coasts of France and Spain. Perhaps she should have it cut short and start all over again. At least she wouldn't look quite so much like a patchwork quilt.

She stood under the rush of warm water, allowing herself to bask in pure sensuous pleasure as she relived that unexpected kiss. Her fingers drifted up to press against her lips experimentally. What had it been like for him? Had he felt the same surge of electricity that had left her both stunned and unsatisfied?

She'd been kissed before, but never had she experienced anything like the touch of Chandler's mouth on hers. It was as if she had been moving toward that one moment in time all her life—as if that one kiss had somehow set a seal on her whole future. And *that* was certainly the most absurd idea of all time!

Wandering downstairs and into the kitchen later on, she suggested to Martha that because Chandler would be going out to dinner and Steve's appetite was practically nonexistent, she might enjoy taking a break. "I can scramble some eggs for Steve and me if you and Mr. Duggins would like to eat out for a change."

"Lawsey, child, I haven't been able to drag that man of mine out to a restaurant since I had a twenty-one-inch waist." The older woman laughed.

"It's your own fault that you still don't. I could founder at the trough on any one of your meals." Belinda helped herself to a sliver of the warm Smithfield ham the housekeeper was trimming. "You and your desserts, and your country hams! I'd all but given up salt and sugar before I came here."

"Go 'way with you! You can eat anything you like and not get fat as long as you have to keep up with that boy. He'd run the wheels off a locomotive."

"Not the way he's feeling now, he won't. I think he might be coming down with a cold."

The housekeeper's reply was lost in the sound of a buzzer. "That's the front door. Chandler's gone off somewhere, and I've got my hands in this ham fat. Will you see who it is?"

Hurrying to the front door, Belinda wondered sinkingly if Mickey or Dick or even Thalia Faircloth had picked a time when Chandler was out to come for Stevie. Opening the door reluctantly, she saw a tall, smiling brunette whose perfectly groomed appearance went a long way toward making up for her lack of true beauty. As a pair of pale-gray eyes took stock of every detail of Belinda's casual appearance, the expectant smile lost a good deal of its charm.

"Is Mr. Harrington in?" the striking woman asked in a well-modulated drawl. Those disconcertingly cool eyes were focused slightly above and to one side of Belinda's left shoulder, making her feel invisible.

"No, I'm sorry."

"May I come inside and wait?" the woman asked in a rather markedly patient tone.

Belinda couldn't see the clock, and her watch was upstairs. She had no idea whether or not Chandler had gone for the evening. Taking her hesitation for acquiescence, the brunette moved past her, removing a pair of black doeskin gloves and slapping them against one palm. She glided—there was no other way to describe her way of walking—into the living room, and Belinda followed helplessly.

Striking a pose in one of the tall windows that overlooked a small formal garden, the newcomer turned to demand, "And who are you?"

Belinda returned the condescending scrutiny composedly. She was not intimidated by the reed-slender figure in handwoven tweed, wine-colored silk, and matching suede boots. "I'm Belinda Massey. I'm here to look after Mr. Harrington's nephew."

The woman continued to examine her with insolent thoroughness. "So they're at it again, are they? For an otherwise sensible man, I sometimes wonder about him.'' Lifting her thin shoulders in apparent resignation, she demanded, "Where is he?"

Belinda did her best to follow the confusion of pronouns and keep her temper at the same time. Gratuitous rudeness she could do without. "Who, Steve?"

"No, silly girl," the older woman drawled, as if explaining a simple point to a backward three-year-old. "Chandler. I would have called first, but I just got back from Phoenix and I wanted to surprise him."

Belinda shrugged helplessly. "Then have a seat, and I'll tell Mrs. Duggins you're here. Maybe she can tell you when to expect Mr. Harrington."

"Oh, don't bother Martha. I'll help myself to a drink, and if Chandler's not here by the time I finish it, then he'll just forfeit his chance to take me to dinner." She made her way across to the liquor cabinet with the ease of someone completely at home in her surroundings, and Belinda marveled at the ball-bearing way her limbs seemed to swivel from her hips. Either the woman was a model or she'd practiced long and hard to achieve that fascinating, reptilian walk. Almost as an afterthought, the svelt brunette glanced over her thin shoulder and said, "You can go now."

And you can go, too—go take a flying leap! Belinda suggested silently as she made her way back to the kitchen. One almost had to admire such highly polished brass. It wouldn't have occurred to that enameled clotheshorse to introduce herself once she learned that Belinda was merely an employee!

"It was a woman," she told the housekeeper, her

expressive voice lifting the latter's sparse eyebrows sky high. "Thin, smart-looking—coal-black hair cut like a man's and eyes the color of a dirty window-pane. She's in the living room helping herself to the Scotch," Belinda finished witheringly. So much for her lovely philosophy of peace and tranquility! It didn't take much vinegar to curdle the milk of human kindness.

Martha inclined her grizzled head as she wiped off the carving knife. "That'll be Enid Smathers, back from that fancy beauty shop out west. Didn't take her long to come snooping after Chandler." Her disdain-ful tone somehow seemed to justify Belinda's instinc-tive antipathy.

"She's a regular visitor, then?" No point in trying to hide her curiosity about the attractive, assured crea-ture who acted as if she had a vested interest in all things Harrington.

"I should say she is, more's the pity. Smatherses and Harringtons have been neighbors for generations, only when Chandler and Bobby went their separate ways a few years back, I thought we'd seen the last of her. Her daddy's been runnin' for the state house ever since I can remember. They never know when to quit, those Smatherses. Think they're God's gift to the Commonwealth!"

A pretty expensive gift, Belinda mused, wondering just where Enid fit into the Thalia-Chandler-Bobby affair. She was certainly stunning, even if she owed her attractiveness more to flawless grooming and an unlimited clothing budget than to any great degree of natural beauty. Furthermore, she seemed perfectly assured of her welcome.

"Quit sneaking that ham, Belinda, or you'll not eat a bite of supper," Martha chided, as if Belinda were no older than Steve. It occurred to her that the housekeeper would use the same tone of voice on her employer, should the occasion demand.

Martha washed her hands and dried them on her commodious apron before going to speak to Chandler's guest, and Belinda wondered whether to rejoin the two women in the absence of a host. Before she could decide either way, she heard the slam of the front door followed by Martha's muttered, "Good riddance."

Anyway, it was time to wake Stevie if she hoped to get him to bed again at a reasonable hour that night. She was there to look after him, and not to entertain his uncle's guests, she reminded herself forcefully. It was going to be hard enough to walk away from those two Harrington males without getting herself involved any deeper.

Steve was fussy enough so that she hadn't time to worry over what she was going to say to Mickey that evening. She managed to get two bites of scrambled eggs into his petulant little mouth and then spent almost half an hour trying to distract him from wanting to watch a favorite television show. Chandler didn't encourage his watching, and for once Belinda was in agreement with him. The child was too highly strung, and now he was more fractious than usual.

She wondered if part of the reason Chandler discouraged his nephew from watching television might

be because of the publicity about the custody battle—if that's what it was. He hadn't volunteered any
information, and she was certainly in no position to
ask. Mickey might have news—perhaps they were
planning to meet with lawyers and settle the thing
once and for all.

In which case, who would win? And to what end?
In just one short week, Stevie had become very dear
to her, and for all Chandler seemed to be the villain
of the piece, Belinda knew instinctively that he was
blameless. On the other hand, Thalia was the child's
mother. Surely that counted more?

Maybe she'd better just get out while she could.
Let someone else decide who was right and who was
wrong—let someone else chase ducks and bake cookies and make up nonsense songs with Stevie. She'd
recover—she had in the past.

And let someone else smooth the wrinkles from
Chandler's forehead? Feel the strength of his arms?
Share the compelling magic of a kiss? Her eyes
clouded over, the gold flecks for once subdued.

By nine o'clock the hands on her watch had slowed
to a crawl. Even the second hand took several minutes
to complete one circuit. She had packed her suitcase
and unpacked it again, and now she was dressed in a
comfortable blue pants outfit, a handwoven shawl
thrown across the love seat in readiness for her dash
down to the gate.

There had been time to think—too much of it—
since she had put a fretful Steve to bed again. She'd
come to the conclusion that she couldn't remain there
one more hour—nor could she leave. Whether on ac-

count of the small boy who aroused all her maternal instincts, or the man who aroused a totally different set of feelings, she was stuck there as surely as if there were bars on all the windows and doors. What she was going to tell Mickey, she had no idea. Perhaps it would depend on what he had to tell her.

At ten minutes to ten she threw the shawl around her shoulders and slipped quietly downstairs. Steve was sleeping heavily, and the Dugginses had taken advantage of the evening off to go to a church social, an affair Martha confessed she had missed since Chandler had moved back home.

A full moon had risen by the time Belinda reached the ornate front entrance, and she pressed her cheek against the cold metal and watched the ragged, iridescent clouds play hide-and-seek across its surface. She heard a car and recognized the patched muffler of Mickey's elderly automobile. As an undercover man, he left a lot to be desired.

The car door slammed with a tinny thud, and then he was on the other side of the gate. "Hi, Bel! How goes it?"

"You make a great private eye! I could hear you coming five miles down the road."

"What did you expect me to do, swing in on a wisteria vine in black tights and a cape? Come on, Bel, let's go sit in the car. We don't want to risk rousing suspicion."

"I don't know who you think is going to see you," she grumbled. "You didn't bring along that agent of Thalia's, did you? How about a publicity shot of the poor, grieving mother reaching through the locked gates? Maybe we could get Chandler to glower for the press—he does it extremely well, you know."

"You sound a little strung out, honey. Is the kid a real pain?"

"Don't call him the kid! His name is Steve, and he's a wonderful little boy—or he would be if he had half a chance." What was wrong with her? She was normally so placid. Now, for some reason, she wanted to strike out at something—or cry her silly eyes out.

"Hold on, Bel. Before you start chewing my head off, let me fill you in on what's happening, all right?" Mickey's tone was placating. "Harrington had dinner with Thalia tonight at her place. They might be ready to negotiate. According to—"

"Negotiate! *Negotiate!* You make it sound like some sort of a business deal! This is a child you're talking about—a real, live little boy with—with big, sad black eyes and a—and a *puppy!*" Her fists were clenched on her thighs, and her eyes were burning from the tears she refused to shed. She'd deal with this thing in a cool, calm manner if it killed her.

"All right, all right, Pretzel, slow down."

If the teasing nickname was supposed to sweeten her up, it failed. She had had it up to *here* with so-called adults who played with a child's life as if they were trading baseball cards. "And you're no better than they are," she flung at her brother. "How can any mother be so careless with her child as to allow him to be kidnapped?"

"Then you think he should stay with the uncle?"

"I didn't *say* that." Taking in a great gulp of air, she made a deliberate attempt to think logically instead of emotionally. If only her nerves weren't so raw from trying to come to some decision on what was best for Steve. And to make things worse, she kept tripping over her irrepressible feelings for Chandler. It was like being in a maze, or a house of mirrors. "Look, what's she like? I mean, what's she really like under all that glamour? I read an article several months ago, but it didn't even mention her husband or her son. It was all about some French actor who hired a sculptor to do her in marble."

"I take it you mean Thalia," Mickey said dryly. He sighed heavily and reached for a cigarette. "I'm beginning to wonder myself. Dick's hooked on her. I wouldn't be surprised if he hasn't been carrying on a one-sided thing all these years, but Thalia?" He blew out a stream of smoke. "Hard to say. She looks like champagne and Chantilly lace, but I kinda get the feeling she's being pushed around by that agent of hers. Giles Ebon—now there's a real shark for you. He's probably already figured out to the penny just how much this whole hassle will be worth on her next contract."

Belinda took a minute to consider his evaluation. It helped to think that Steve's mother wouldn't deliberately exploit him. Still, if she were so weak as to allow her agent to do it for her, was that any better? And anyway, was that what this was all about? Wasn't it a case of Chandler's thinking he was better suited to raise the boy than the child's own mother was?

They were leaning up against the elderly yellow station wagon, never having made it inside. "Oh,

Mickey, I don't know—I just don't *know*," she wailed, leaning against her brother to bury her face in his neck. "Why did you ever get me mixed up in this mess? Now, I'm trapped—I can't just walk out and leave him, and I can't explain that I came in the first place just to see if I could help steal him back for his mother. Chandler would hate me if he knew that! He's the most honorable—the most decent—"

Mickey patted her back awkwardly. "Come on now, baby. I didn't mean for you to go getting your-self all involved. You aren't going to be much use to me if—"

"*Use* to you! Is that all you can think of?" She pulled away, staring up at her brother as if he had suddenly sprouted horns. "You're no better than any of the rest of those—those vultures! Well, I'm stay-ing. I don't care what you say; I'm not leaving that child to be pulled apart by a bunch of—"

She spun away, suddenly aware of the glare of headlights that illuminated them clearly. The sound of Mickey's car door slamming reached her only dimly, and when a moment later the yellow station wagon roared off in the opposite direction, she was still standing there, frozen by the rapid approach of the other car. Not until it was almost upon her did she jump to one side, nearly coming to grief in the hawthorn hedge that fronted the brick wall around the estate. Her shawl was snatched from her shoulders by thorns, and belatedly, she covered her face and backed away. She heard a car door slam. No tinny thud this time; it was a solid thunk, and it had been slammed with considerable force.

In the confusion that followed, she could hear Chandler's harsh voice, and then his hands came down on her shoulders like steel talons, turning her to face him. "Stop pulling on me, my pants are caught on a thorn!"

"Are you all right?" he demanded tersely. He made short work of extricating her from the shrubbery, and then he yanked her into the revealing beam of the headlights.

"I'm all right, for Pete's sake! Just go away and leave me alone." She'd sooner have landed in a barbed-wire fence than to have to face Chandler. He was furious, and she was still hopelessly confused; if he started asking questions, she just couldn't take it.

Chandler slid his hands up under her arms and lifted her bodily into the car. "Of all the harebrained—you little idiot! Don't you know better than to jump out in front of a car that way? I almost hit you!"

"Well, you didn't," she retorted angrily, as her various scratches and abrasions began to make themselves felt. "And anyway, I didn't jump out in front of you—I jumped out of the way. What did you expect me to do, wait there?"

He slammed the door and strode around to the driver's seat, not giving her the opportunity to even consider escaping. By the time he was seated beside her, his hands gripping the steering wheel as if to keep them from going around her neck, her anger had begun to simmer down. It was her own fault—not Chandler's. Her own stupidity. She opened her mouth to offer a grudging apology, and he shut her off with a terse demand.

"Would you be so kind as to tell me what you were doing out here at this hour of night? Or shouldn't I ask?" He swore harshly under his breath and snapped on the interior lights to glare at her ravaged face.

Defiantly, she refused to turn away. Her hair was a wild tangle, her face blotched from the earlier outburst, and on top of that, she felt as if there were scratches on every available surface of her skin. If he had just come back from being with Thalia, he'd be amused at the contrast, no doubt.

"You look like the very wrath," he growled, contempt blistering her already ragged ego. "It's a shame I had to come back early and break up that tender little scene beside your boyfriend's car." His eyes bored into her painfully. "Well, you can steam up as many back seats as you want to once you're through here, but I'd appreciate it if you'd restrain yourself while you're still in my service."

She took it in dogged silence. Facing him across the few feet of soft, leather upholstery, she let the words wash over as she willed herself not to respond by so much as a flicker of an eyelash. She was guilty, all right—her face must be telling him that much—only not of what he was accusing her. How could she tell him that her own conscience was punishing her enough without his help? She couldn't let it show— couldn't let him know how badly she was hurting.

She'd always been aware of his air of thinly veiled arrogance. It was an integral part of his magnetic appeal, only now, when he was under so much tension, it became a highly dangerous quality. He could have no way of knowing how long a different sort of tension had been growing inside her; only a fool would have built on the fragile foundation that had been laid six months before. The relationship that he had thought founded on mutual trust and integrity had crumbled before it had had a chance to grow, and if she hadn't been so utterly drained already, she could have wept.

Her silence severed the last link in the chain that held his temper in check. Belinda recognized it the instant it happened. He grabbed at her shoulders and shook her until her hair fell over her face. "Speak to me, dammit! I won't *tolerate* your insolence."

"You won't have to." Her voice was flat, expressionless, and she struggled against a strange sense of inertia as she willed herself to feel for the door handle.

He reached for her again, and in jerking away to escape him, her head cracked against the doorframe. A small cry left her colorless lips. Instantly, she was pulled against him, her face pressed tightly to the hard worsted surface of his chest. The same detached inertia still held her in its grip, and she closed her eyes, oblivious to everything except for the unexpected comfort of his arms.

"Why don't you *say* something?" he groaned into the tangle of her hair. "Don't let me do this to you." It was almost as if he were pleading with her to escape him, but she hadn't any more strength. Too much had been expended battling with her own guilt, with Mickey, and with the same compelling attraction that now held her immobile.

"If you had to see him—" He broke off abruptly.

"Do you love him so much? Is that why you couldn't stay away tonight?" It wasn't the words that made her pulses flicker like summer lightning, but the slow, rhythmic feel of his hand on her back, sliding the thin fabric over her skin.

She struggled for an answer. "I—it's not what you think, Chandler."

"You don't love him?" One of his hands had found its way under the weight of her hair and was caressing her nape, fast erasing all rational thought from her mind.

"Of course I love him," she blurted helplessly, "but that's not—"

"No, it's not," he said flatly, his fingers taking on a new hardness as they slid under the loose jacket and the camisole she wore under it. "It's no reason to deprive us both of what we both want. You're an adult, in spite of that deceptive look of innocence." His hand moved around to her breast, touching, caressing with incredible sensitivity as well as an expertise that had her gasping tremulously.

"Chandler, please…"

"Don't stop me, Belinda. I need you—you've been growing in me like a fever." His hands lifted to capture her face, and he turned it so that the light of the full moon shone down on it. His eyes in shadow looked oddly hurt as they moved slowly over her features. "Maybe it can make up to both of us for other…disappointments tonight," he finished bleakly.

The words were a sudden icy deluge, and she drew back. He allowed her her freedom just so far and no farther, shifting his position so that he was half reclining. Before her sluggish mind could react, he recaptured her and stilled her struggles by tangling one hand in her hair to pull her down on top of him. "I ought to have my head examined for starting something out here—" His mouth was making nibbling little forays along the tendon of her throat. "We both belong in my bed, and the sooner the better, but..."

Before she could twist away, his mouth was on hers, his tongue probing for the acceptance she was determined to deny him. "All right, we'll play it any way you want to," he growled against her stubbornly sealed lips. He shifted her so that she lay between his thighs, holding her with an iron gentleness when she began to struggle. One hand slipped up to her breast, and his fingers began circling her nipples with feather-light touches, tormenting them into aching erectness until she ignited from the heat of his arousal.

Her moan was the release he sought. He took swift advantage of it, thrusting his tongue past her guard and using its invasion with telling results. She found herself moving in mindless harmony with the rhythm he set until, with a harsh expletive, he pushed her from him, holding her boneless body suspended for agonizing moments before practically hurling her away from him.

Numbed, she watched as he raked an unsteady hand through his hair. "I'm too old to be making love in the front seat of a car," he rasped, his hooded eyes slowly regaining focus. Without even looking at where she lay, half collapsed against her door, he switched on the ignition and aimed the silent, powerful Cadillac through the open gates, not stopping to close them behind him.

She was out of the car before it came to a complete stop, not waiting, even when Chandler called after her. The front door was unlocked—another bit of irresponsibility on her part, she supposed, but she was glad now she hadn't bothered to lock it after her when she had dashed out earlier. Racing up the stairs, she was intent only on gaining the sanctuary of her room. She *had* to pull herself together enough to get away from there before she made a complete fool of herself. *A little late for that!* The thought was accompanied by a hysterical desire to laugh.

When her door opened, she was standing frozen in the middle of the sitting room where she'd stopped just minutes before, hands clasped to her cheeks, eyes staring blindly at the half-shuttered window.

"What are you playing at, Belinda?" Chandler demanded with quiet forcefulness.

Turning, she caught sight of her reflection. She looked haunted—utterly pallid except for the bruised shadows that had blossomed under her eyes as her natural color receded. It had always been that way. She registered stress by fading instantly into a colorless little wraith.

"I'm sorry, Chandler. I have to go. Now—tonight, if possible."

To her acute discomfort, he continued to study her from his position near the door. Those pitch-dark eyes that could direct a beam clear through her were completely unreadable as he said, "You're not going anywhere, Belinda. I stepped out of line tonight. For that I apologize—extenuating circumstances on both our parts, I suppose. It won't happen again."

"I know it won't because I won't be here. Chandler—I *have* to go." She was pleading with him, pride a commodity she could no longer afford. There was little enough pride left to her, anyway, and if he discovered her real reason for being there, even that would be gone. Except for the occasional social invention to spare someone's feelings, she'd never lied in her life—couldn't lie, according to her brother, without guilt being written in mile-high letters across her expressive face. In this case, she had slipped obliquely around the truth until she was sickened by her own duplicity. Others might be every bit as deeply involved in whatever farcical plot she had been drawn into; that was their own fault. She had to live with herself and she wasn't sure she could, knowing she had deceived a child.

"Why?" he asked starkly.

Her eyes fell. "I can't tell you that, Chandler. Just let me go—please."

At his continuing silence she lifted her gaze again and was shocked by the look of utter defeat she saw on his strong features. He was tired; she, of all people, knew the tremendous tension he must be under, and there were bound to be other pressures she knew nothing about. She had seen him look this way before—gray, almost haggard—but now it was as if he had reached the limits of even his enormous strength.

"What will I tell the boy? He's grown attached to you in the short time you've been here."

She flinched. "I know. I—it works both ways. Believe me, Chandler, I wouldn't go if I had any other choice."

He shrugged, his hand on the door as he prepared to leave her. "A matter of priorities, I guess. You have your own life to lead." Laughing harshly, he added, "A man my age should know better than to—" He broke off with a half-stifled oath. "Shall we put it down to a particularly frustrating evening for both of us? Accept my apologies, my dear. Your young man will come around soon enough." He smiled grimly at her blank look. "Oh yes, it was clear enough that you had words. I saw you kiss him, then jump back. He drove off like a demon. These spats aren't all that serious, give it time."

Reaching out impulsively, she took a step toward him. "Chandler, please—let me explain."

Even as he mocked her with a cruelly self-derisive smile, she knew it was futile. What could she explain, after all? Nothing that would build a bridge across the abyss that separated them.

Shrugging in defeat, she turned away and then lifted her head again at a sound of distress from the bedroom across from hers. "It's Stevie," she muttered, the hopeless tangle of her personal affairs forgotten.

Chandler was one step behind her as she hurried through the dressing room, switching on the light automatically. "Oh no—angel, don't," she crooned, kneeling to take the groggy child in her arms. His bed was ruined, his pajamas reeked of vomit, and he was burning up with fever.

Chapter Five

Four days later Belinda massaged her temples and wondered if she had the energy to prop her eyes open another minute. The doctor had come and gone twice. Trust the Harringtons to manage a house call; *she* couldn't even arrange an appointment for a three-thousand-mile checkup. That first time Martha had stayed with Steve while Belinda and Chandler had stepped outside the door to hear the verdict.

"Virus, I expect," the little man had muttered into his Vandyke beard. "Bad one going around—watch out you don't all get it. High-strung child—some signs of malnourishment." Both Chandler and Belinda had been shocked by this pronouncement, but the doctor had gone on to explain in his nervous, bird-like manner that it was a case of too much junk and not enough plain, nourishing food. "Give him soups and salads and fruit. Make him eat cornbread. He'll get used to it. I'd be on the lookout for signs of spastic

colon if he remains in a stressful situation. Bring him
in later on when he's steady on his pins again and
we'll give him a thorough going over.''

Belinda had no time to worry about later; her hands
were too full of now. Sometime during the ordeal of
around-the-clock nursing, she became aware of a
quiet presence. Chandler's was the supportive
strength that enabled her to stay night and day in
Steve's room, bathing, soothing, changing bedclothes
and trying to get liquids down his parched little throat.
It was Chandler who brought up her meals and then
stayed with her to see that she ate them when eating
was the furthest thing from her mind. And it was
Chandler who more than once plucked her asleep
from the bedside chair to carry her to the other twin
bed in Steve's room, slipping off her clothes and covering her with a light spread; Chandler who gathered
up each day's pile of soiled linens and carried them
to Martha, returning with a fresh supply. He forced
her to walk outdoors, or simply to sit in the garden,
for at least an hour a day when she would much rather
have collapsed on the spare bed.

She had asked him once if they couldn't find someone to come in and help with the extra laundry, but
he had shrugged helplessly. ''Martha has a built-in
resistance to extra help—you're the one exception.
It'd be worth my life to bring in anyone new.'' His
tired smile had invoked an answering one from her.

The second night, when Steve's feverish thrashing
had demanded both their attentions before he settled
back into a fitful sleep, Belinda had found the courage
to broach the subject that had been on her mind al-

most constantly. "Don't you think his mother should be notified?"

At first she took the instant stiffening of Chandler's features for anger, but it dawned on her that it could be guilt instead. "I think you can safely leave that decision to me," he replied evenly.

She was too tired to bother with diplomacy. "If you want my opinion, you have no business trying to look after a five-year-old boy. You don't have time to do play with him—you don't even take the time to get to know him." Beyond discretion, she warmed to her subject. "A child needs to know he's wanted, Chandler! He needs to know that someone loves him no matter how naughty he's been. Do you know that Stevie can't even run in your house? He has to tiptoe around this old museum to keep from breaking any of your precious treasures. Well, let me tell you something, that's no way to bring up a growing boy!"

"The devil with this house!" Chandler exploded, raking a hand through his already-rumpled hair. "Do you think I don't love the boy? Good God, Belinda, what more can I do? I took him out of an environment I thought was ruinous and brought him here for his own good. You heard the doctor—the boy wasn't even getting decent food! The idiots Thalia hired to look after him didn't care what he ate—or *if* he ate. At least he gets decent food here, and as for the rest of it, what do you think you're here for?"

There was no answer to that. As far as Chandler was concerned, she was there to look after his nephew. As far as Mickey was concerned, she was there to spirit the child back to his mother if they couldn't settle their differences otherwise. And she? Heaven help her, she was there because she couldn't bear to walk away and leave this irascible, impossible man!

The day Steve demanded to see his puppy and threatened a tantrum when Belinda tried to put him off, she knew the worst was over. Stray virus, intestinal flu, or whatever, it had been rough on him. It had been rough on them all. Chandler, not surprisingly, looked almost as haggard as poor Steve did, but Belinda knew that the aching misery inside her own heart had nothing to do with any virus.

She'd learned a lot from the child's feverish babbling, and more from Martha's outspoken comments. "That Thalia tried to get her claws into Chandler before she ever met Bobby. Better for that poor babe upstairs if she'd managed it, too! At least Chandler would have been man enough to keep her out of trouble. Poor Bobby—for all he was a lovable boy, he was ever a wild one—six years younger than Chandler and spoiled by every female that ever laid eyes on him, including his own mama, rest her soul."

So she'd been right. She hadn't misinterpreted that greedy look Thalia had given her brother-in-law that evening six months before. As if that weren't enough, Martha also launched in on Chandler's relationship with Enid Smathers.

"She'll have him, too, sooner or later. There'll not be any children from that match, I can tell you. That woman's got no more human warmth to her than that broom over yonder!"

"He must see something in her," Belinda ventured dismally. "She's awfully smart-looking."

"Smart-looking, pshaw! She's efficient, he says. Whenever I try to get him to make some decision about the house, it's 'Ask Enid this, ask Enid that!' If you ask me, the poor man plain doesn't know any better. Thinks as long as his meals are on time and his shirts are starched just right, that's all a man needs in this world. Well, I could tell him better, even at my age!"

Belinda didn't want to hear any more. She had to escape before she gave herself away. Forcing herself to speak calmly, she said, "Martha, if you can hold the fort while I shower, I'll help you in the kitchen later on."

Chandler had brought the puppy into the library and was keeping an eye on Steve down there while the two women cleaned up the sickroom. That done, Belinda felt she could steal a few minutes for herself, a few minutes to come to terms with a truth she had avoided facing for too long.

What had happened to all her common sense? What good had her hard-earned education done her? She stared at her image in the bathroom mirror. Her looks had hardly been improved by the four-day ordeal, especially since she'd started at ground zero. Odd how the matter of that devastating episode after she had left Mickey had been completely submerged in the emergency—or not so odd, at that. A man of tough integrity, Chandler would never allow personal matters to intrude on his duty. He was one of the strongest, most caring men she had ever met, and loving him was probably the biggest mistake of her life.

Her wet hair twisted up in a towel, she was stepping into her jeans when Chandler tapped on her door and called to her. "Belinda, are you decent?"

"Give me a minute," she said breathlessly, tugging the zipper over the hollow of her abdomen. The jeans hung on her. She must have lost pounds in the past few days. She reached for one of the three shirts she had brought with her and jerked it over her head, dislodging the towel. The door opened and she clutched the wet towel, the unbuttoned pullover shirt, and the sagging jeans in her hand. "I *said* a *minute!*"

"Sorry." His eyes were everywhere, enigmatic as only black eyes can be. "I wanted to know if you had enough strength left to go out to dinner tonight. It would do us both a lot of good to get out of the house."

The idea alarmed her as much as it appealed to her. Her heart was pumping like a fire hydrant, and she seemed unable to tear her eyes away from him. Dressed in flannels and a crew-necked pullover of navy shetland, he seemed younger in spite of the deep furrows that grooved his lean cheeks and the sprinkle of gray that was newly evident in his thick, glossy hair.

"Sure—if you want to."

"Dr. Harrington's surefire prescription for overworked young gentlewomen," he said, his teasing baritone drawl devoid of the sarcasm she half expected.

"I'll have to change."

His eyes followed the course of her long legs, lifted to the purple cotton shirt that was twisted about her waist, and he smiled at her. As she melted in her tracks, she was reminded that she had seen that rare and precious smile no more than half a dozen times, at best. "Not for my sake," he said, "but I'll wait if you want to dry your hair. Can't have you coming down with the same vicious bug that bit poor Steve. Martha will stay with him while we're gone. It's already arranged, and before you ask," he teased gently, "I've taken care of the damage the pup did. Soap and water, a little sandpaper and varnish, a touch of glue, and you'll never know the difference."

"What broke? No—don't tell me about it! I can't stand it," she wailed. And then, "Are you sure? I mean about going out?" Her eyes were far more expressive than she knew, and he nodded, moving to the love seat.

"Take all the time you need. I'll see you in five minutes."

It was a heady, supremely foolish thing to do, and she was going to relish every minute of it. Later, crossing the James River Bridge in the plush automobile, she stretched her legs out in the roomy space under the dashboard and pressed her back into the creamy soft leather upholstery. She'd almost forgotten what it felt like to wear nylons and high heels. The swirly paisley skirt and turtleneck top were not really dressy, but she had always loved the outfit, considering it one of her most flattering.

Chandler must have called ahead for reservations.

It was the sort of place where the proprietor knew his clients and greeted them personally. There were no menus; Chandler, with characteristic assurance, ordered first and consulted with her later. Not that she could find anything to criticize in his choice of bouillabaisse topped with an incredibly light puff pastry, crab Norfolk, and a salad of marinated artichokes, spring onions and mushrooms. There was a sweet potato pudding afterward, topped with heavy cream, and there was wine with each course.

She tried everything. She wasn't going to waste a single particle of sight, sound, or taste. Every word, every look, each inadvertent touch of those long, beautifully formed hands was tucked away in a secret compartment of her heart.

Belinda asked about Chandler's work. Oddly enough, she had no idea what he did each day when he drove off.

"I'm a naval architect," he said with quiet pride. "I design sailboats for pleasure and larger, strictly utilitarian vessels for a living."

The discussion of his work led to an argument about the feasibility of wind as a modern source of ship power. From there they went on to discuss their mutual love of sea stories and science fiction, and Belinda regaled him with some of her more memorable escapades as a child growing up on the upper James River.

"My—" She had almost mentioned Mickey. As all the problems she had left in York County rushed back to confront her, some of the brightness seemed to go out of the evening, and she reached for her purse. "I guess we'd better be going," she murmured. "It was so lovely—just for a little while I almost forgot..." She let it go, her voice more wistful than she realized. Nor did Chandler attempt to prolong the outing. Outside again under a warm, damp sky, he took her hand, and the gentle, undemanding pressure of his fingers restored her enough to smile at him.

"Happy?" he murmured.

She nodded. "Mmhmm. Disgustingly, gluttonously full," she said candidly, "but happy."

"Good." He ushered her into the car and maneuvered them out of the parking lot, but something in his tone of voice made Belinda turn to study his strongly defined profile.

"How come I suddenly feel like the condemned man after his last meal?"

"Perceptive little creature, aren't you?" His grin was slanted her way, even though his eyes remained on the narrow band of highway.

"I should have known there had to be a catch," she groaned. "I'd have felt better if we'd settled for burgers and fries. As it is, I have a feeling I'm going to pay dearly for every single calorie I consumed tonight at your expense, and I *don't* mean by gaining weight!"

"You could do with a few pounds. We put you through the wringer, didn't we? Have I thanked you, by the way?"

Turning away, she stared at the fleeting countryside, just now beginning to unveil its pastel finery. "You pay my salary." She shrugged. "I don't need any special thanks." She hadn't meant to sound quite so ungrateful; it was her guilty conscience, emerging after recently having been buried under the avalanche of around-the-clock nursing activities.

"There are some things that can't be bought," he observed quietly.

Her reaction was instantaneous. "I'm sorry, Chandler. That sounded churlish, and I didn't mean it that way. Maybe I don't consider that I rate your special thanks. After all, I was only doing my job." It *still* wasn't coming out right! Oh, blast Mickey for involving her in this mess in the first place.

As if her unspoken thoughts had triggered his memory, he said, "By the way, there were a couple of calls for you. You were sleeping both times, and I didn't want to wake you—Lord knows, you've lost enough sleep."

She didn't want to hear it. Not now—not while she was still able to hold together a few of the threads of magic.

"The boyfriend again—Mickey. The message was the same both times."

There had been a brief rain shower while they were in the restaurant, and now the sound of the radials humming on wet asphalt formed a monotonous background noise as she waited for the ax to fall. It must be all over if Mickey was sending her messages through Chandler. "Well?" she prompted irritably when she could stand the drawn-out silence no longer.

"I'm sorry, Belinda. I don't know what the fight was about between you two, but I know you'd hoped to patch it up once things settled down and you were free to meet again. I'm afraid the mess in my own personal life has spilled over and ruined yours."

"Chandler, what did he *say?*"

"Just that everything was all over. His exact words were to 'tell Bel that it's over. She's free now—and that she'd understand.'"

They pulled up into the circular driveway in front of the house, and Chandler switched off the engine and turned to face her. "Belinda—maybe I can help. Maybe if I talk to him—" His voice was strained, as if the words were being forced from him, and when he added gruffly, "Any fool who'd drive off and leave you that way doesn't deserve you," she felt as if the breath had been pressed from her body.

At least she had sense enough to keep her face hidden. She stared at her fingers as they traced the pattern on her skirt, knowing darned well her eyes would be glowing like headlights—and with no more reason than a few kind words, spoken carelessly in an attempt to offer comfort.

"Belinda? You're not crying?" His hand captured her chin, tilting it so that the light from the house shone full on her face and there was no way she could hide from his concerned gaze. She watched, mesmerized, as he leaned closer, his stern mouth softening until she ached from pure longing. She met him halfway.

It was as if he couldn't get enough of the taste of her. It was as if there was a world of ideas to be shared in the pitifully finite space of a single kiss— as if they couldn't say enough with the urgent joining of mouth against mouth, and were afraid of saying

too much. *I'm imagining things,* she thought frantically as one by one the cells of her brain shut down.

Chandler gripped her knee, and she could feel the
tension in his fingers, the force of his holding back.
And she didn't want him to hold back, didn't want
him ever to let her go again. He lifted his face. Her
eyes opened reluctantly, and she watched him with-
draw. Not physically; he was still so close she could
feel the heat of his body, breathe the particular blend
of sandalwood, wool and healthy male flesh that was
so distinctly Chandler.

This withdrawal was something more intangible,
but every bit as real, and she wanted to fight it,
wanted to hold onto him with both hands and keep
him from shutting her out. There was nothing she
could do. He had closed himself up in that impene-
trable shell that confounded all her efforts to reach
him.

"If you need me, I'm here," he said, and she could
have kicked him.

"I don't, but thanks for your noble offer of self-
sacrifice." And then she could have kicked herself.

He reached past her to open her door. "I'll put the
car away and come in the side door. Are you afraid
to go in by yourself?"

"Of course not," she said with a calmness that hid
the fact that she was crumbling into ruins inside.

By the time she had scrubbed the light makeup
from her face and changed into her pajamas, she'd
recovered somewhat, but she was still in no condition
to sleep. It would have to be either hot milk or a
dozen rounds of sun salutes before an open window.

The thought of going down to the kitchen and possibly encountering Chandler was out of the question. Before she could face that event with equanimity she was going to have to get herself in hand.

Paradoxically, the series of asanas, or yoga exercises, she performed each morning to bring her into a relaxed state of alertness was equally effective for keying her down enough to sleep. She opened the window in her sitting room. The shutter was still half-closed, waiting for Pete to return from spring break, but the air that flowed in was soft and rich with the scent of newly plowed fields, wild onions, and burgeoning buds. There was something especially poignant about this particular season just now. She felt an odd restlessness that had nothing at all to do with the recuperating child, or the muddle she seemed to have made of her personal relationships.

"The nesting urge," she muttered under her breath, and she applied herself resolutely to repeating the twelve-position routine once more. She was at rest, standing in the middle of the floor, head back, arms limp at her sides, when the door opened and Chandler entered unannounced, uninvited.

He apologized before she could gather her wits to eject him, but not before she had seen the touch of alarm, interest, and then something decidedly sensual flicker across his features. "Are you all right?"

"Of course I'm all right!" she snapped. "Did you think I was about to fling myself from the window onto your precious boxwoods?"

"I give you credit for a little more consideration than that. For your information, there's a gable window in the attic that opens over the Japanese quince—they're thorny, but they don't take quite as long to grow back as the boxwoods."

Disarmed by the totally unexpected touch of his humor, Belinda dropped to the love seat, suddenly exhausted, both emotionally and physically. "Seriously, Chandler, what is it? Steve?"

He sat down beside her, and she tucked one bare foot up under her. She could have wished for her robe—not that there was anything seductive about a pair of white lawn pajamas. All the same, she was acutely aware of her own naked body underneath the thin fabric.

"You mentioned paying for all those calories. I've come to collect. No—" He laughed, the sound tinged with bitterness. "Not the way you're thinking. I've learned to control my more—ah—lecherous impulses." He grinned, and this time there was no hint of the bitterness—only a rueful self-mockery that she found unexpectedly touching.

"I don't do windows," she warned him, knowing a desperate need to defuse a potentially explosive atmosphere. He might have *his* libido safely harnessed, but that said nothing of hers!

"Steve's mother is coming tomorrow for an indefinite stay."

Her mouth hung open until he reached out and lifted her chin with his forefinger. "And I need you more than ever. Steve needs you."

"But—"

"But." Leaning forward to prop his arms on his thighs, he stared at an ambiguous figure in the patterned rug. "Let me tell you a little about Thalia. She was Thelma Murdock when she won her first beauty contest at the age of one. From then on she averaged winning about three a year. She was a beautiful child with an ambitious mother—an unfortunate combination in this case. Thelma—oh, yes, the name was changed to Thalia when she was twelve; the Faircloth part was manufactured when she and her mother moved to the West Coast after she graduated from high school. For Thalia, the beauty was a mixed blessing. She was brought up to depend on it to get her anything and everything that struck her fancy. And it worked—up to a point."

Belinda's foot had gone to sleep, but she didn't dare move. Chandler had never before broken the mantle of reserve he wore like a second skin. He was an extremely private person, and she knew instinctively that he was confiding in her things he had never told anyone else about his sister-in-law.

Once more reading her with uncanny accuracy, he said, "I'm telling you this for a purpose, Bel." She thought he must be unaware of having used the diminutive. Mickey had always called her that—that or Pretzel, after she took up yoga. "Later, Thalia couldn't come to terms with the fact that she was just one of thousands of beautiful faces for hire. She made a few movies, landed a television role or two, and in the process discovered that she was practically devoid of talent. Her ego couldn't handle it. It's led to—well, that's another matter. But to put it bluntly, Belinda, she's never grown up."

"Where does that leave Stevie?"

"In your very capable hands, I devoutly hope," he pronounced quietly. "Thalia needs time and care before she'll be ready to take responsibility for either herself or the boy. She's alternately used and abused him. No," he said to her look of dawning alarm, "not that sort of abuse. Benign neglect might be a more apt term. She thought of him as a doll, played the modern madonna bit until she grew bored with it, and then, after she and Bobby separated the first time, pushed him off on whomever happened to be handy."

So they had been separated, and more than once. That explained a lot, Belinda thought—but not enough.

"Unfortunately, she's under contract to an agent who's totally unscrupulous, and she hasn't got what it takes to break free. I blame Ebon partly for the breakup in the marriage. Not that Thalia and Bobby were blameless. Both were immature, and Bobby was as stubborn as Thalia is weak."

He grew silent, and Belinda waited patiently, her eyes taking liberties with the way the hair grew down onto his nape, the beautiful shape of his hands, his wrists. He turned to her before she could harden her glance and something moved behind the surface of his eyes, something that had her unconsciously leaning toward him.

Rising abruptly to his feet, Chandler reached up a hand to massage the muscles at the back of his neck. "As much as I hate it, I've got to be in Washington tomorrow morning. A meeting with some Navy brass that can't be postponed. As for Thalia, she'll probably be late, as usual, and I can't wait. I've asked a neighbor, Enid Smathers, to look in. Martha says you've met Enid. She and Thalia are good friends, and if anything comes up that you or Martha can't handle, Enid can deal with it. Meanwhile, I'll be back as soon as I can.'' He lifted a brow and waited for any questions, and because she couldn't pick one out of the logjam, she remained silent. "No questions? Good. It'll serve the purpose of keeping your mind off that idiot who walked out on you, at least. Believe me, Belinda, you're better off without him. One of these days you're going to meet a man who'll appreciate the special qualities that go to make up Belinda Massey.''

She couldn't help herself. "Which are?''

He grinned down at her. "Which are a beautiful mind and a beautiful character to go in that very beautiful body of yours. And don't think I'm not uncomfortably aware of every one of them—especially the last.'' His eyes grew bright with intent. "Which makes this one of the more stupid things I've done lately,'' he said, reaching for her.

Fully aware of her own rashness, she went into his arms willingly, reaching her own up around his neck when he gathered her to him. She lifted her face, eyes closed, lips parted in readiness. When nothing happened, she opened her eyes in bewilderment to glimpse an undecipherable look on his lean, somber face. Almost reluctantly, as if to put an end to her speculation, he placed a kiss on each eyelid and then traced the contour of her cheek to the corner of her lips.

Unable to fight the heady compulsion, she shifted

her face so that her mouth covered his. With a soft groan, he opened his mouth to her. Wresting the control for himself, he guided her deeper and deeper into a kiss that recklessly fueled a fire that was already raging out of control. She was incredibly aware of the growing tension of every muscle, every hard sinew in his body.

Glorying in her corresponding softness, she swayed in his arms, pressing her breasts against his chest as she willed his hands to caress them. When she felt his palm slide down her back and under the elastic of her pajama pants to curve down over the cool flesh of her hips, she drew her breath in sharply between her bared teeth, shattered by the devastating urgency that gathered like a tightly coiled spring inside her.

"Ahh, no, no," he groaned a moment later against her throat. Even as she felt the desire that surged through his powerful body, she could sense his growing rejection moments before he actually put her away from him. He held her by the shoulders, as if aware that she hadn't the strength to stand alone. "Sweetheart, I can handle celibacy well enough," he growled ruefully. He stood clear of her, allowing his arms to drop to his sides. "I'm just not at all certain I can handle the sort of temptation you're presenting, and at the moment, I'm in no condition to test myself."

Chapter Six

In spite of the rich food and the hopeless confusion of her emotional state, Belinda slept soundly. It was well that she did. Steve recuperating was three times the handful that Steve stricken had been. Chandler left before nine, mentioning going by his offices before heading north. She didn't even know where his offices were. He went *some*where every day when he left home, and if she'd been hitting on all eight cylinders she might have realized that a man of Chandler's stature didn't conduct his business affairs from a rosewood desk in the library. He was just such an exasperatingly private man!

Before he left he stopped by her suite. She had been making the beds while Martha gave Steve his breakfast downstairs. "I didn't hire you as a maid, Belinda," he said, frowning as she pushed a stray tendril of hair from her forehead.

"I didn't offer myself as a maid, but the stairs

bother Martha. She really should have someone to help her." Her eyes went to the soft leather overnight case he carried. He looked every inch the successful businessman in a three-piece suit of shadow-striped slate gray. "Do you have everything you need? I should have asked."

If it were possible for black eyes to darken, his did. "Stop it, Belinda! If I needed a wife to look after my affairs, I'd have one. Just see to it that Thalia stays put here and keep Steve out of her range as much as possible. I hate to have to be gone at a time like this, but Enid can cope with anything that comes up. By the way, I've locked the liquor cabinet. If you want anything from there, Martha knows where the key is."

Why not lock up the silver, as well? Belinda glowered silently.

He left her before she could explode. Hands on her hips, she waited until she heard the front door shut firmly, and then she gave vent to a series of highly inventive oaths before bursting into tears.

Five minutes later she picked herself up, scrubbed her face ruthlessly and finished smoothing the spread on Steve's bed. The rebellious monologue that raged inside her head veered erratically from Chandler's smug assumption that she was his to order about to the unfairness of his attack on her motives.

"'I didn't hire you as a maid, Belinda,'" she muttered with pious mimicry. "Do this! Do that! 'Enid can cope!'" She snatched the towels from the bathroom and flung them at the hamper. "'If I needed a wife to look after my affairs, I'd have one!'" Her bottom lip trembled threateningly. "Well, you can bet your beeswax *I* wouldn't be in the running."

"Did you say something, Belinda?" Martha called from the head of the stairs. Belinda could hear her puffing all the way from the bedroom. Together they got a room ready for Thalia Faircloth Harrington, and before the finishing touches were quite completed, the sound of her arrival could be heard.

During the next few days it seemed to Belinda as if she doubled her age. Twenty-five years of relatively trouble-free existence that included helping her elderly parents pull up stakes and settle into a new home and caring for several children in a foreign country had left her unprepared for dealing with a cantankerous five-year-old, an immature thirty-year-old, and a beautiful if bloodless socialite whose role seemed ambiguous, at best.

Thalia arrived by taxi. It seemed that her driver's license had been recently revoked, and for once her spectacular looks had worked no miracles. Duggins and the smitten driver carried her luggage—three large white leather suitcases and a queen-sized makeup case—to the second floor. Belinda, recalling a few of her own hassles with surly drivers who seemed glued to the seat, looked on with dry amusement. She wondered if Thalia would recognize her as being connected with the Lovatt-Massey Agency, but she needn't have worried. As far as the stunning actress was concerned, Belinda was a mere walk-on, if not just a part of the scenery.

Thalia, her clear blue eyes unexpectedly childlike

in her skillfully made-up face, confessed that since Chandler had forbidden her agent even to call her and hatefully dismissed her personal maid, she was glad to find someone around besides the housekeeper. "You wouldn't believe the grief I got the last time I was here over a simple thing like a cup of coffee in the morning!"

It was the following day before Belinda discovered that the "simple cup of coffee" was a full pot, freshly ground and freshly made, accompanied by two slices of thin, dry toast and a glass of just-squeezed grapefruit juice, all delivered to the bedside at precisely nine-thirty in the morning. She had also discovered that Thalia alternately smothered her small son with affection and ignored him, that she was about as tidy as a cyclone, and that she *adored* clothes, *adored* pasta and *adored* soap operas, all seemingly with equal fervor.

The first tantrum came when she discovered the liquor cabinet was locked. Summoning Martha with an air of commanding authority vaguely reminiscent of an old Joan Crawford role, she demanded to be given the key. The housekeeper pretended to have misplaced it, and there followed a scene that left the older woman red-faced and indignant, the younger one ruining a generous application of mascara, and Belinda both disgusted and puzzled.

A television set was ordered installed in the elegant living room. After that, from roughly eleven in the morning on into the afternoon, the house was relatively peaceful. Belinda amused Steve with quiet games and short walks with the puppies rolling along beside them. He seemed totally unconcerned with his mother's presence, taking her mercurial moods for granted with a mature acceptance that brought an ache to Belinda's throat.

Enid Smathers glided onto the scene about four o'clock on the second day of Thalia's stay. In deference to the warm, springlike weather she wore ivory silk and a matching cashmere cardigan instead of handwoven tweed and suede. Belinda let her in, since Thalia was lounging in the living room, engrossed in one of the soapier soaps. Still wearing a hot-pink negligee that should have clashed wildly with her hair but didn't and a pair of marabou and satin mules, she looked utterly out of place in the rather spare, understated elegance of the formal room. The handsome fruitwood end tables were littered with nail-polish bottles, cigarette ashes, tissues, and magazines of the sort Belinda had always considered trash.

"Hullo, darling," the tall, sophisticated brunette drawled, her eyes radiating a sort of malicious amusement as she took in the scene with one sweep of her cool gray eyes. "You do spread yourself around, don't you?"

"Oh, Enid. What are you doing here?" The redhead sounded petulant.

Belinda decided her presence was superfluous and headed for the kitchen, where she had left Steve draped across the scrubbed worktable "helping" Martha form cloverleaf rolls. She swatted the child playfully and started gathering up the utensils to wash.

"The Smathers woman?" Martha asked, her thinned lips indicating her opinion of the visitor.

"In person. I left them to it."

"Just as well. I'd sooner be caught in the middle of a cat fight myself." Then, catching Belinda's meaningful glance at Steve as he concentrated on shaping a grayish blob of dough with his small fingers, she shook her head and set the pan to rise on top of the warming oven.

A few minutes later Thalia's mules could be heard clattering up the front stairway, and Enid appeared at the kitchen door to announce that she was taking the actress home with her for the evening. "My father's away and there's no point in my dining alone. Especially since there's no one here."

Ouch! Belinda nodded her acknowledgment, deliberately avoiding Martha's glance. She'd been patronized before, but never, perhaps, with quite such stylish carelessness.

Her ego completely intact, she hid her amusement and watched in reluctant admiration as the tall, thin woman swiveled her negligible hips and drifted away. "I'll bet she walked miles with a book on top of her head when she was a little girl," Belinda murmured when they were alone again.

"If she were my daughter, she'd need that book in another spot!"

Belinda laughed and swooped Steve up for half an hour of fresh air before she started fixing his early supper. She was teaching him a few of the simpler yoga positions. So far he'd managed an unsteady, leg-waving shoulder stand, but his ambition was a perfect headstand.

By the time she'd settled her charge for the night and watched both local and network news she was bone tired. Keeping up with one small dynamo was a full-time job, without having a spoiled, lazy houseguest to cater to. Martha would have managed after a fashion, but it was plain to anyone with half an eye that the poor woman should have been retired years ago. Either that or Chandler should have insisted that she have help.

Staring dejectedly at her last clean pair of jeans—she'd been so busy "rinsing out a few things" for Thalia that she had forgotten her own—reminded Belinda that she had meant to call Mickey about sending out some clothes. She dialed the apartment, and after several rings, the phone was answered by the agency's girl Friday.

"Massey residence, Jones speaking."

"Shelvie, it's me, Belinda. May I speak to Mickey?"

"Oh, hi, Belinda. He's not here. He and Dick are testifying tomorrow in the MacElrath thing, and they're out trying to locate Symington."

Belinda, who had never heard of either Symington or MacElrath, nor did she want to, asked impatiently when he was expected back.

"Gee, how would I know? He was griping about not having a clean shirt to wear to court tomorrow, so I thought I'd do a load of laundry for him. This place was unbelievable by the time I came back—from the office, I mean."

Belinda groaned inwardly. She was no neatnik, but Mickey was a dead loss. "Do me a favor, Shelvie. Rake a path to my room and throw a few outfits into a suitcase—you know the sort of thing. Jeans, tops, a skirt or two and the yellow cotton dress in case this weather holds up. I'll either have someone pick it up or get Mickey to send it out in the next day or so."

"Will do. Ah—how long do you think you'll be staying out there?" Shelvie's husky drawl held a curious note. "Mickey says you weren't doing so hot in the job market until this thing came up."

"Oh, boy! Well, I can't go into it over the phone, but let's just say I'm gainfully employed for the moment, thanks to the Rover Boys."

That done, she took a long, luxurious soak and then, in her cotton pajamas with her hair in a braid, she practiced the Smathers ball-bearing glide, watching her reflection over her shoulder. Finally, with a snort that was part laughter and part disgust, she knelt, lowered her head and clasped it in her arms. Stiffening her legs, she walked herself up and into a headstand.

Thalia was sleeping heavily when Belinda took up the breakfast tray; wrinkling her nose, she cracked open a window and backed out again, leaving the tray on a table in the stuffy room. Not only was the place a shambles, with clothes, magazines and makeup scattered on every surface, all liberally sprinkled with cigarette ashes and bath powder, but the room smelled like a cross between a beauty salon and a distillery!

Shortly after noon Belinda heard a crash from the

front of the house. Glancing out to where she had left Steve playing with his puppy under the budding cherry tree, she saw that he hadn't moved from the spot. "I'll see what it is," she murmured distractedly to Martha, who was putting lunch on the table.

Thalia, in a tea rose slip lavish with handmade lace, was standing in the middle of the small living room, staring vacantly at the shards of a Chinese porcelain flambé-glazed jar that once sat on the burled elm chest. The actress, her fiery hair in wild disorder, turned quickly at Belinda's soft gasp.

"It's all your fault! If you hadn't made him hide the key, it would've never happened."

Alarmed, Belinda took in the pouched eyelids, the smeared makeup, the tear-streaked petulance. "Hide what?" she asked, bewildered.

Balling her small hands into fists, Thalia shook them in an important gesture of fury, reminding Belinda of Steve in the throes of one of his temper tantrums. "It's not *fair!* He *knows* I need something to calm my nerves. He's got no business hiring someone like you—a guard to watch me every minute, as if I—as if I were a..." She broke off in a storm of weeping, rubbing her eyes in a childlike manner.

Belinda moved swiftly and led the distraught actress to a chair, patted her consolingly on the shoulder, and set about picking up the broken pieces. Perhaps there was an expert somewhere who could put them together again—all she could do now was collect them and put them aside. She was considerably more worried by the irrational behavior of the noisily sobbing woman, and as soon as she had retrieved the last splintering bit and put it, along with the others, on one of Thalia's lurid screen magazines, she turned to face her.

"If you'll stop crying long enough to tell me what's wrong, then maybe I can help you," Belinda said in her most reasonable tones. It wasn't the first time she had had to deal with such behavior, but as a rule, the culprit had been a good deal younger.

Thalia sniffed loudly and turned a ruined face up to her. With the badly smeared mascara, she resembled a small, angry raccoon. "*You* know! You probably put him up to it. Enid said you'd do anything he asked to keep from getting fired."

And Enid would know, of course, Belinda thought rancorously. The wonderfully efficient Miss Smathers, who could cope with anything. Well, let her cope with this awkward, embarrassing situation. Belinda had been hired to look after one child—not two! Aloud she said, "Miss Smathers was mistaken, whatever she led you to believe. I don't know anything about a key, but I suspect you're just hungry. If you'd like, I can bring you a light lunch in here, or you can have it in your room. Maybe you'd feel better after a warm shower, hmm?"

A few more resentful sniffles and the miserable woman allowed herself to be led away. Was that what it was? Belinda mused as she helped her up the stairs—alcohol? No wonder poor Chandler had his hands full. And his precious Enid obviously didn't bother to keep her own liquor cabinet locked.

Treating the actress much as she would a child, Belinda got her showered and dressed in a flowing red silk caftan and led her back downstairs. She switched on a soap opera and left, returning shortly afterward with a tray of soup and salad and a glass of milky iced coffee. "I'll just give your room a little attention, Miss Faircloth. If you need anything, call me. I'll leave the door open."

During the course of the day there were two more tantrums and several wild accusations, all of which Belinda took in her stride. No wonder Chandler had told her to keep Steve away as much as possible. It couldn't be good for the child to see his mother in this condition.

Belinda puzzled over whether or not she should tell Chandler about Enid's dereliction of duty. She hated telling tales—nor did she particularly want to be the one to disenchant him over his paragon of efficiency. As to that, he might not even believe her. He'd known and trusted Enid all his life, according to Martha, and if he knew how Belinda had come to be there in the first place, he wouldn't be inclined to take her word for the time of day.

She cleaned and aired the bedroom, trying all the time to convince herself that she was overreacting. Enid had probably served wine at dinner, and maybe a little something afterward. As closemouthed as Chandler was where his private affairs were concerned, she might not even know that there was any problem. Meanwhile, there was nothing Belinda could do, even if she had the authority. It would take more cunning than she possessed to deal with a determined alcoholic, especially when she had her hands full keeping up with Steve. Chandler would be home any time now. He could take over the whole difficult situation.

Enid arrived shortly before eight to take Thalia to dinner again. "Any company is better than none," she declared with typical tactlessness. Belinda half expected the volatile redhead to fly into another tantrum at the implied insult, but Thalia was all smiles as she hurried upstairs to get ready.

Sauntering over to the burled elm chest, Enid moved a jade figurine an inch to the right and adjusted a lampshade. "You know, of course, that she's an alcoholic," she drawled to Belinda. "Why Chandler insists on having her here, in spite of the fact that neither Thalia nor that child of hers can appreciate a place like this, I'll never know. It took me ages to get it back in order again after the last visit."

Irritated by such a callous attitude, Belinda said, "But I thought Miss Faircloth was a friend of yours."

"Miss Murdock"—she stressed the name—"is Chandler's sister-in-law. An unfortunate state of affairs, but then, Bobby *would* marry her, and the Harringtons have never shirked their duty. Considering our relationship, I naturally do all I can to make it easier for Chandler."

Of course you do, you pit viper, Belinda seethed inwardly. "Did Miss Faircloth have something to drink when she was with you last night?"

"My dear girl, what possible business is it of yours? I'm not a jailer, you know. The sooner Chandler reconciles himself to having the poor thing institutionalized, the better off we'll all be. Meanwhile, he depends on me to keep her from being bored to death with no one here but that wretched brat and an old woman for company."

Belinda soared to past the point of anger. She came all the way around to a strange sort of admiration, not untinged with amusement. Poor Thalia, if this was the best she could do for entertainment. "By the way, which category do I come under, wretched brat or old woman?"

Enid's eyes registered a vague puzzlement, and Belinda quickly controlled her bitter amusement. Evidently, she was too negligible for consideration. "For Chandler's sake, I hope you can manage to keep Miss Faircloth out of trouble until he gets back."

Enameled eyebrows moved smoothly aloft on a porcelain forehead. "Re-ally, I think you can leave that to me. And while we're out, would you please do something about this pigsty? It should never have been permitted. Do you know what nail polish does to the finish of fine furniture? And the carpet? That happens to be a genuine Shirvan, you know."

Belinda turned with relief to see Thalia hurrying downstairs, an anxious smile on her freshly made-up face. "Made it in record time! I'm just thrown together—if my makeup man could see me now, he'd have a fit. Belinda, you will keep an eye on my baby, won't you? And don't wait up," the actress trilled gaily as she waited by the front door for Enid. "I never know what time it is when I'm having fun!"

Watching the taillights disappear down the drive, Belinda smothered a feeling of guilt under a fresh surge of indignation. Why should she feel guilty just because Thalia was going to be allowed to drink as much as she wanted? If Chandler's perfect woman didn't consider herself a jailer, Belinda certainly shouldn't, especially as she hadn't even been told of the problem. That emotionless clothes horse was probably doing all she could to advance the day when poor Thalia was tucked away in some sanatorium! And then what? Would Stevie be dealt with as efficiently? That creature didn't have blood in her veins—she had freon!

Once more Belinda was asleep when Thalia came home. She'd done her best to stay awake, but the long day's activity, with its attendant emotional workout, was too draining. Besides, as cowardly as it seemed, she didn't really want to know the state of Thalia's sobriety—or the extent of Enid's culpability.

Chandler returned just before eleven the following morning. A warm, restless wind had blown up out of the southeast, promising showers before too long, and Belinda had taken Steve outside to work off some of his endless store of energy before they were housebound again. They'd run about, swinging from limbs, jumping over imaginary hurdles and throwing sticks for the puppies until Belinda was ready for a break.

"Do Yogi Bear!" Steve chanted when they flopped down on the grass beside a low wall. He persisted in calling the simple asanas she had taught him Yogi Bears.

"Have you ever seen a stork?"

"You mean that brings babies?" he asked innocently.

"We'll tackle that one some other time," she murmured dryly. "I mean the big bird that builds its nest on top of people's chimneys." She went on to relate all the storklore she knew and then stood up to demonstrate. Instinctively searching out the flattest surface, she hopped impulsively onto the rock wall. "Watch this," she cried gaily, kicking off her shoes. Lifting her arms over her head, palms together, she raised one knee outward and placed the sole of her bare foot against the knee of her other leg. The wind lifted up her flowered cotton skirt and flung it around, and she laughed aloud, feeling the first few sprinkles of rain on her upturned face.

She stood there for perhaps a full minute while Steve lurched around in an uncoordinated attempt to mimic her. A gust of wind swirled dust and dried leaves around her, and she closed her eyes, laughing from the pure joy of her healthy young body.

"Uncle Chandler!"

Startled, Belinda flung out her arms for balance, opening her eyes to see Chandler Harrington standing at the edge of the pecan grove. She felt as if she had just swallowed her heart! He was frowning—even from a distance she could see that he looked terribly tired, as if he hadn't slept since he had been gone.

Steve scrambled up and ran, followed by all five puppies, to throw his arms about his uncle's knees, but it was at Belinda that the man continued to stare. She dropped lightly from the wall and felt for her shoes, never once taking her eyes from his lean, unsmiling face. "Hi," she called softly, tentatively. "Welcome home."

And then, as if she had imagined it, the oddly intense look was gone. Chandler's hand rumpled Steve's hair and he swooped to lift one of the dogs.

"We'll have to see about finding homes for these fellows. They're growing up."

"Pup can bite a stick," the child announced proudly. "Wanna see?" He found a twig and hurled it a few feet away. "Fetch, pup! Go get it!"

Belinda poked along behind, feeling unaccountably neglected. Chandler hadn't rebuffed her so much as simply ignored her. Surely he had gotten over whatever small thing she had done to annoy him before he had left.

At the door, Steve raced past them, and Chandler stood aside politely for Belinda to follow. Trying valiantly to school her expressive eyes to hide the bewilderment she was feeling, she smiled with a spurious brightness. "Did you have a good trip?"

He nodded briefly. "Where's Thalia?"

"In her room, I expect. She wasn't awake when I took her breakfast in, but she'll probably be coming down for lunch in a few minutes."

"There've been no—incidents, then?" His voice was cool, detached, but his eyes were strangely watchful.

Perhaps that explained his coolness, she rationalized wistfully. It was embarrassment. It would be hard on a man with Chandler's inherent pride to have to ask for help with a problem of that nature. "Nothing really serious," she said as tactfully as she could. "Miss Smathers has been around a lot." Which was as close as she intended to come to indicating anyone.

Chandler's sigh of relief would have gone unnoticed by anyone else. Belinda's every nerve was so closely attuned to him that she was aware of every flicker of expression on his lean, strong face. There was a pallor underlying his naturally dark complexion, a weariness that showed itself in his slightly reddened eyes, in the way his hand reached up frequently to brush against his forehead. There was even a flush on his cheeks, confirming Belinda's impression that he was embarrassed.

"I'd like to see you in the library after lunch, Miss Massey," he said curtly. Miss Massey! Belinda reeled inwardly at the totally unexpected formality. Then it *was* something she had done.

Lunch was a strained affair at best. Martha informed them when they came inside that Thalia had a headache and would have something later on in her room. Steve chattered unceasingly, and Chandler was distracted to the point of eating nothing at all. Belinda's eyes seldom lifted to the level of his face, but she couldn't help but be aware of the way he pushed his food about on his plate. Whatever her transgression, it was serious if it was affecting his appetite to this extent.

Of course, he was obviously tired. She knew his meeting had concerned the design of a fleet of supertankers to be built at Hampton Roads, and coming on the heels of Steve's flu, it was enough to erode his normally even disposition. Or was it?

He had discovered how she came to be there! It *had* to be that. Just how, or when, she had no idea, but there was nothing else that could account for the sudden change in his attitude. He'd been angry even before he left. There had been that gratuitous remark about not needing a wife.

Utterly confused, Belinda poked at her food, her appetite gone. Somehow he had discovered her identity and was furious at himself for being taken in. With a feeling of dejection, Belinda led Steve up to his room for a nap, taking her time washing his hands and face. She settled the child, lowered the shades and braced herself to go back downstairs.

Nice while it lasted. She tried vainly for an air of bravado. Oddly enough, now that her departure was imminent, she felt little pain—only a defeated sort of numbness.

Outside the library door, she paused, hearing Chandler's terse voice on the phone. Only when he hung up with a forcefulness that boded no good for her interview did she rap timidly on the door.

"Come in, Miss Massey." It was more a command than a request, delivered in a tone that must have left his tongue frostbitten!

He *did* look dreadful. Part of her wanted to soothe that feverish-looking flush from his face and another part wanted to run for cover. "You wanted to see me, Mr. Harrington?" she asked, her stiff voice barely audible. He looked absolutely formidable, scowling abstractedly at the phone that way.

"All right, what do you have to say for yourself?" He lifted his stern gaze to rake her hair, still windblown from her earlier session outdoors, and her eyes slid guiltily away. The contempt was plain on his face, and she knew its source. Even so, what she had done hardly warranted quite such wholesale condemnation.

"You must take me for a complete fool," he rasped. "If I hadn't had so much on my mind at the time, I'd have remembered immediately."

Belinda stared at him, bewildered. One of them wasn't quite making sense, and she didn't think it was herself. "Mr. Chandler, I know I shouldn't have—"

He broke through her indignant outburst as if she hadn't spoken. "I should have known better. Thalia must have had a willing, even eager, ally in you. Of course, Enid warned me about leaving you in charge, but I assured her you were thoroughly dependable, levelheaded and completely to be trusted in all—"

Numbness gave way to outrage as Belinda listened to his description, placing her own interpretation on it. A placid, insipid little nonentity! She took a deep breath, ready to describe in loving detail the cold fish who had no doubt twisted facts around until Belinda was responsible for Thalia's fall from grace.

Once more Chandler cut her off, storming at her in a manner that was totally out of keeping with his normal composure. He seemed almost to have forgotten she was there.

Belinda allowed her own fury to escape in a defeated sigh as she took in the red patches on his high cheekbones, thrown into relief by the unnatural pallor of the rest of his face. His eyes glittered like anthracite and his voice was hoarse with anger. She couldn't argue against such a concentration of wrath. Instead, she found herself irrationally wanting to smooth the

deep furrows from his forehead, massage the tension
from those broad shoulders.

"If I'd had any idea who you were when you came
here, you can be certain I'd never have hired you to
look after my nephew—much less my sister-in-law!
It's a case of hiring a thief to catch a robber." He
laughed shortly, and the sound made her wince.

"Well, you can *un*hire me easily enough! Believe
me, I can do without playing nursemaid and drudge
to a woman who should be old enough to look after
herself! And as for taking orders from a pigheaded,
insensitive clod who has about as much feeling as
a—as a—"

She was on her feet. The gold flecks in her dark-
green eyes were glinting dangerously as they collided
with Chandler's obsidian glare. Her face by now
would be as pale as his, she knew from past experience, and she'd be looking her very worst. Stress always did this to her, and this was stress of a degree
she had never dreamed of, much less experienced.

Chandler's voice hardly registered as she gathered
her forces to flatten him before walking out, and the
phrases that managed to break through her indignant
thoughts were almost incoherent.

"—young girl, no supervision, running wild—"
He went on relentlessly. "Drinking, making a fool of
herself with a bunch of besotted Frenchmen!" She
listened in stunned disbelief as it dawned on her that
he was accusing her of something totally different
than she had thought. Her mouth fell open as he
painted her an irresponsible, abandoned opportunist,
and poor Henri and Georges as drunken, lecherous

creatures dragging her down to a life of depravity—
or vice versa.

"I don't believe this!" she whispered, shaking her
head slowly at the irrational tirade.

"Oh, you wouldn't remember it," he went on bitterly. His eyes were narrowed as he glared at the wall
behind her. It was as if she weren't even present—as
if he were talking to himself. "You were too busy
showing off in that indecent dress, waving your wineglass around while you auctioned yourself off to the
highest bidder, and fool that I was, I'd have outbid
them all! You stuck in my mind like a spur and fes-
tered there, and I couldn't forget you! Only I did,
didn't I?" He laughed harshly, and she flinched. "My
conscious mind pushed you out of sight, where you
couldn't disturb me again, but my subconscious
wouldn't forget."

Horrified, she could only stare at him. "But, Chandler, you don't under—"

With an agonized groan, he lurched to his feet and
strode past her, almost knocking her down as he
rushed to the door and up the stairs.

Chapter Seven

There followed a nightmare that a part of her would treasure for the rest of her life. It had taken no more than the ominous sounds coming from Chandler's room upstairs to send Belinda's feet flying after him. Oh God, how could she have missed it? The doctor had warned them both! All the symptoms had been there, staring her right in the face, and she'd been too wrapped up in her own hurt feelings to see beyond the tip of her nose.

Too ill to fight back, Chandler allowed her to wash him, remove his shoes and socks, his shirt, tie and pants, and put him to bed. After she hung up his clothes and straightened up the bathroom, she went in search of Duggins, quickly outlined the situation, and sent him upstairs to help the patient into a pair of pajamas.

"Oh, lawsey, what on earth are we going to do now?" Martha wailed as her solemn, lanky husband disappeared up the back stairs. Duggins was far more at home outdoors tending the grounds and making minor repairs than he was in the house. In fact, this was the first time Belinda recalled seeing him in any room except the kitchen.

Martha continued to agonize, declaring that at her age she couldn't be expected to do all a body had to do to keep a place so large running. "It's not like it was when I came here as a bride, to work for Miz Rowena, Mr. Chandler's mother. We had good help in those days, not like the girls you get now, that either rob you blind or sass you back. I'll not have another one of them in my home!"

Belinda gave a fleeting thought to the fact that it was, indeed, the Dugginses' home as much as it was Chandler's. She was beginning to realize that far from being reluctant to hire additional help when his housekeeper and yardman reached retirement age, Chandler must have suffered their decreased efficiency in stoic silence rather than hurt their feelings.

With Steve still napping and Thalia nursing a headache of highly suspicious origin, Belinda declared an emergency. She called a war council consisting of herself, the housekeeper and her dour husband, unconsciously assuming command.

"I've already sent for the doctor—he'll be here within the hour—but that's only the beginning. I *think* it's no more than the virus Steve had, but we can't be certain. At any rate, unless Chandler goes to the hospital, which might be better all around, we're going to have to do the best we can under difficult circumstances. I can handle the nursing. Martha, forget

the cleaning and concentrate on the meals and the
laundry. Mr. Duggins''—she couldn't bring herself to
call the elderly yardman by his given name, for they
didn't share the same comfortable relationship that
she did with his wife—''if you'll look after feeding
the dogs and—Pete! Is he back? He could take charge
of Steve, couldn't he, Martha?''

''Not less'n you can reach him on that motorsickle
of his'n and get him back here from the mountains,''
Clarence Duggins told her dolefully.

''Hmm. Well, that's out, then. You don't suppose
Thalia...?'' At the dubious expressions on both the
Dugginses' faces, she hurried on. ''As for our neighbor Miss Smathers, the less I see of that woman the
better I'll like it. I know it's none of my business who
comes and goes, but I'm telling you now, Martha, if
that woman so much as sets foot in this house while
I'm here, there's going to be trouble! We'll have
enough on our hands without having to worry about
her upsetting Thalia.''

''She never!'' explained the outraged housekeeper,
knowing very well what Belinda meant by ''upsetting.''

''Who else?'' Belinda shrugged expressively. ''I
unpacked Thalia's bags myself, and there was certainly nothing there. Of course, I had no idea of the
problem then, but I couldn't have missed anything.''

The laconic yardman, looking slightly claustrophobic, heaved himself to his feet. ''You ladies can settle
it out betwixt you. I'll be around somewheres should
you need me, and I'll see that don't nobody bother
you none.''

Belinda smiled gratefully, taking the triple negative to mean he'd keep the Smathers woman out of her hair for the duration. She discussed logistics with Martha until they were interrupted by the arrival of the doctor. Belinda tiptoed up the stairs ahead of him. Some ten minutes earlier Duggins had reported Chandler sleeping heavily and now, relatively confident that somehow the rest of the household would continue to function, she determined to devote all her energies to his recovery.

With Dr. Timmons's assurance that Chandler suffered from nothing more serious than exhaustion and the virus that had lately filled the local hospitals to overflowing, some of the tension that had braced her back until it hurt drained away, leaving her feeling strangely limp. She was to keep him cool as his fever mounted, change the linens as soon as they became damp and get as much liquid nourishment in him as possible once his angry stomach would accept food again.

"The nausea usually tapers off after the first day or so, but he'll have a severe headache," the doctor warned her as he handed her a vial of tablets. "And he'll be raring to get up long before he's ready. Keep him down, young lady. I don't envy you the job, but you'll probably wind up with a broken leg to nurse if he tries to get up too soon. The boy bounced back in less than a week, but Chandler's been driving himself for too long. Sit on him if you have to, and call me anytime, night or day."

Chandler was sleeping heavily again when she stepped back into the bedroom. She had adjusted the shutters so that air could flow freely without too much sunlight. In his feverish condition, his eyes would be sensitive. After carefully moving a wide, tobacco-brown armchair closer to the bed, she allowed herself the luxury of studying his gray face to the extent that she began to feel vaguely guilty. He'd be furious if he happened to wake up and catch her at it, but she wasn't about to waste her opportunities. Especially since it was probably the last time she'd ever be able to stare at him that way.

His nose looked prouder than ever in spite of the unhealthy color that had replaced his normal tan. Long and straight, it bisected his lean face with an arrogance that ironically struck her as endearing. His brows were incredibly silky in spite of their being thick and dark, and his lashes were both long and dense. Her wistful gaze skimmed his hollowed cheeks and the square, slightly jutting jaw to rest on his mouth. In repose, it lost much of its sternness. She swallowed convulsively as she fought back the desire to kiss those sensuous, sensitive lips. "Just once before I go, I'm going to take advantage of that man," she promised herself in a whisper that could hardly have reached his ears.

Nevertheless, he stirred restlessly and mumbled something unintelligible. Belinda moved silently to his side, laying a hand on his forehead. Touch was no sure indication of temperature; she knew that very well. Even so, she couldn't keep her hand from lingering there, and as he settled back into a deep sleep, she mouthed the words, *I love you.*

With an armload of damp linens, she slipped out of the bedroom several hours later, heartily grateful for the Red Cross home-nursing course that had taught her to make a bed with a patient in it. Chandler had roused enough to cooperate when she told him to roll over, but he was inclined to be obstinate, sick as he was. Fortunately, she was just as obstinate.

Thalia peered out her bedroom door, looking ever worse than the patient. It would be the last straw if she should come down with the virus, too.

"What's everybody creeping about for?" she asked plaintively. "I told Martha an hour ago that I wanted something light to eat, and you wouldn't believe what she said to me—she told me to hush up and behave myself, as if I was no older than Stevie!"

"Chandler's sick," Belinda said tersely. She had no patience with self-indulgence at the best of times, and this was hardly that. "Martha has all she can do to handle regular meals and the laundry. If you want something to eat in between, then you'll have to get it yourself."

Looking incredibly injured, the bleary-eyed red-head stared at her as if she had been ordered to cook a banquet for a hundred. "Well, I *do* have a headache," she began. "A teensy-weensy little drink..."

"No *way*. Look, Thalia, I'm as sorry as I can be for your problems, but at the moment, I have all I can say grace over. You'll just have to grow up. It's about time you began to take responsibility for yourself and your son, anyway, unless you want him to grow up to be just as weak as you are."

When the beautiful, ruined face began to crumple,

Belinda could have kicked herself. It wasn't like her to be cruel to anyone, particularly someone whom she considered to be weaker. "I'm sorry, Thalia. I honestly don't know what got into me. If you'd like, I'll make you a sandwich and a cup of coffee while the washer's filling for these."

Very much on her injured dignity, the actress drew herself up haughtily and declined the offer. "I'm perfectly capable of making my own lunch, in spite of what everyone thinks." A cunning light entered the guileless, pink-rimmed blue eyes. "Maybe I'll just phone Enid. We might go out for an early dinner."

Inventing wildly, Belinda told her that Enid Smathers had called to say she was leaving town unexpectedly; at the same time, she made a mental note to unplug all phones except for the kitchen extension and the one in the Dugginses' quarters.

"Oh," Thalia murmured pitifully, her shoulders sagging in defeat.

It was well past dark by the time Belinda found time to get herself a bite of dinner. Someone must have taken care of Steve, for when she dashed to her own room for a quick shower and a change of clothes, she glanced in to see him sleeping peacefully, a large plastic aircraft carrier in his arm.

Martha was nowhere in evidence, but there was a pot of fresh string beans cooked with tiny kernels of corn, and a plate of ham biscuits in the oven. Belinda poked about in the refrigerator and uncovered a bowl of sliced cucumbers and onions in vinegar and helped herself to a generous serving.

Taking her plate back upstairs, she curled her legs up in the commodious chair and consumed it all without taking her eyes off the sleeping man beside her. Several times during the night she dozed, waking each time Chandler moved. Toward dawn, he grew restless, muttering and flailing his arms as she tried to soothe him. Once when his hand struck her on the side of the face, she held it to her cheek, allowing her lips to touch his palm before she carefully lowered his arm again. Tears wore a crooked path down her cheeks as her heart filled to aching fullness with conflicting emotions.

Oh *God*, how much she loved him! It was totally unreasonable, totally hopeless, and yet she savored every moment of it, the pain as well as the sheer glory of loving. If, by some miracle, she ever cared at all for another man, it would be a poor imitation of what she felt for Chandler.

"They say suffering builds character," she murmured huskily to the unheeding man. "One of these days, my beloved, I'm going to be the most formidable dowager this country's seen in a long, long time."

The doctor paid a quick, reassuring call the following day just before lunchtime. Martha showed him in, lingering at the front door for a word with her husband, who seemed to have assumed the duties of keeper of the gates. Flexing a foot that had gone to sleep, Belinda stood to greet the dapper doctor, answering a few low-voiced queries after he had examined the patient.

By the third day, Chandler's fever had broken and his disposition had worsened to the point where Belinda considered asking for combat pay. There had been no sign of Enid Smathers, nor was she about to ask Duggins if there'd been an attempted visit. Surprisingly enough, she'd seen Thalia and Steve together several times, and although the actress had glared at her accusingly, she had soon turned her attention back to her son. Just before dinner, Belinda hurried downstairs for a pitcher of diluted fruit juice—Chandler *hated* it, but he was dehydrated enough to drink anything. Thalia and Steve were lying on the floor exclaiming over the exquisite figures of an antique chess set they had found on a shelf in the library.

"Look at this, Belinda," the redhead said eagerly. "All these carvings—it's *got* to be genuine jade. And look at all these tiny bits of onyx—did you ever see anything so cute? I wonder which one of the old pirates brought this home with him."

Cute was hardly the word Belinda would have applied; nor would she have referred to any of the shipping magnates whose grim portraits cast a pall over the foyer as old pirates. Nevertheless, she was delighted to see Thalia and Steve obviously enjoying something together. Maybe there was hope for their relationship yet.

Belinda continued to ignore her patient's nasty disposition. She swabbed him down with cool, damp towels, refilled his ice cap, and practically force-fed his depleted system with nourishing liquids. She'd taken any amount of verbal abuse and grinned irreverently at him, glorying in her brief moment of possession.

"You're a real tyrant, aren't you?" he asked weakly, after downing a mug of strained soup.

"How sweet of you to say so." She opened the window and pulled the sheet up over his chest. He pulled it back down to his waist, and she calmly reached for a sweater. "If you insist on catching pneumonia before you're even over the flu, kindly wait until you've found yourself another nurse. I don't think I could take another siege of your nasty disposition without resorting to a little gentle torture."

"Have I been bothersome?"

She eyed him disbelievingly. "Bothersome? Now why on earth should you think that? Just because I mentioned calling the National Guard a few times—"

His laugh was a weak parody of itself, and she clenched her fists behind her back to keep from reaching out to him. "Ah, Belinda, I've shattered all your illusions, haven't I?"

"Illusions, Mr. Harrington? You mean all that twaddle about the Southern gentleman, the strong, silent he-man? The invincible hero mystique? Oh, deah me, *no*, Mr. Harrington!" she simpered. "How could you think a thing like tha-yat?"

He laughed, then groaned, and she handed him his freshly filled ice cap. "Later, Belinda," he whispered raggedly. "I'll settle up with you later."

Her laughter faded, and she wondered dejectedly how far back the account would reach.

Then, having slept through the better part of four days, Chandler was once more ready to get up and

take charge of the universe. For four days Duggins
had practically had to carry him to the bathroom, but
now that he was beginning to get his strength back,
he questioned Belinda demandingly about everything—his phone calls, his mail, Thalia and Steve. He
insisted she bring him all mail, all newspapers, as well
as the portable television, and she put him off with a
promise of "the next time I go downstairs." He was
cross, but no more so than any impatient, imperious
man who had been unexpectedly laid low by a virus
that was no respecter of persons.

Interestingly enough, he seemed to have forgotten
all about the calamitous battle they had been involved
in when he had succumbed. Belinda wasn't fool
enough to think the reprieve could last. The reckoning
would come soon enough; Chandler had promised her
that, but even in his weakened condition he now knew
that Martha couldn't manage alone.

On the fifth day, along with his dinner tray, Belinda
brought up the stack of mail that had come to the
house, but she refused point-blank to call either of his
two partners to have the mail sent out from the office.
"Try this soup," she urged in a tone she might have
used on Steve. "Martha made it especially for you."

It *had* to be accidental, but his gesture of annoy-
ance caught Belinda on the arm, sending the spoon
flying across the bed and causing the tray to slide to
the floor.

Her lips tightened as tears of pure frustration
burned in her glittering eyes. She was exhausted. It
had been another long day after a short night, and she
had changed the linens less than an hour before while

Chandler had been showering—his first solo attempt since he had started taking solid food again. All the sponging while his fever raged, and the perspiration after it had broken, plus his perpetual restless thrashing about had kept the washer and dryer running almost around the clock, and now this.

"Do you know what I'd like to do to you, Chandler Harrington?" she fumed.

Looking absurdly shamefaced, he shot her a cowed, sidelong glance, and she proceeded to tell him exactly how much satisfaction it would give her to put him across her knee and whale the living daylights out of him.

"Do you know what I'd like to do to you, Belinda Massey?" he inquired softly, a suspicious glint in his eye.

She glared at him balefully. Reaching across the bed for the spoon before she began to clean up the mess on the floor, she didn't bother to answer. When he caught her wrist and gave it a sharp jerk, tumbling her across his chest, she yelped and did her best to scramble out of his reach.

"I'll tell you what I'd like to do to you," he grinned, and he whispered in her ear while she struggled to regain her balance. "But until I get my strength back," he continued, "I'm afraid we'll have to settle for this."

This was a kiss that caught fire from the first instant, leaching the strength from her bones so that she found herself being drawn unresistingly up onto the bed beside him. Hands that had lost none of their firm decisiveness manipulated her until she lay halfway across him, her face held down to his. She couldn't have moved if she had wanted to. And to her fleeting dismay, moving was the last thing on her mind.

As if hungry for the touch of her, his hands were everywhere—tangling in her hair to angle her head for his pleasure, moving the layers of her clothing aside to explore her body avidly, as if he were a starving man and she offered his only hope of sustenance. His lips moved to her throat, and she twisted her head back on his pillow to give him better access, groaning when his tongue flickered in the hollow at the base of her neck. "Chandler, you've got to stop this," she whimpered helplessly, not wanting him to stop at all.

His lips paused on their journey southward to smile wickedly. "Dr. Timmons assured me I'm no longer contagious, *Bellefleur*—but if you do catch my bug, I claim all nursing rights. I owe you a few indignities." His tongue caressed the pale slope of her breast before moving on to tantalize the proud pink summit with slow, electrifying circles.

Within seconds, his heart was hammering thunderously beneath her, and she gave a fleeting, concerned thought to his depleted condition. The nurse was quickly submerged in the woman, however, when he reversed their positions, rolling over to lie on top of her. "You have on too many clothes, *ma belle*," he murmured against her lips. He had already divested her of her shirt, and because she never wore a bra, that left alarmingly few garments between them.

"Chandler, you mustn't," she pleaded unconvincingly. Her body was writhing helplessly beneath him by now, totally out of contact with her brain.

"Unbutton my shirt," he commanded, lifting his upper torso so that her trembling fingers could unfasten the pajama top she'd insisted he wear. The movement brought the full weight of his hips onto hers, and her whole world was centered achingly in the small area of contact as she felt the thrust of his powerful masculine need. His pajama top dispensed with, he found the drawstring of her gathered pants, and she fought down her impatience as he fumbled awkwardly.

Once the drawstring was loosened, his hands sloped down over the cool ivory of her hips, cupping, caressing, shaping her to his powerful desire. "I've dreamed of this," he muttered into the tangle of her hair, "fantasized about having you here in my bed, with all the time in the world to make love to you." His tongue found the flat pink shell of her ear and he interspersed kisses with fragments of love words, causing a rush of chill bumps to break out all along her body.

"Chandler—Chandler, you're driving me crazy," she gasped. "Feel what you do to me." She took his hand and slid it down her flank.

His breath was a jagged sound, his voice harsh and curiously flattened, and he took her hand and guided it. "Now feel what you do to me," he rasped. "I'm not sure just who started this, my tyrannical little darling, but—"

And then, *"Damn,"* he muttered impotently, collapsing his full weight on her, the task unfinished.

She could have wept. All common sense had long

since fled, leaving her selfishly resentful of his inability to seduce her.

Seduce! If the truth were known, there was no seduction involved. All her carefully guarded moral scruples had flown out the window the first time she'd seen him—or if not the first time she had seen him, then certainly the first time he had touched her.

Since then, she'd come to love him with every atom of her being. And loving meant giving—and giving meant receiving. And she wanted to give far more than he was in any condition to receive at the moment.

"I'm sorry, love," he muttered into her shoulder. She could hardly breathe with the weight of him bearing her down into the mattress, but not for the world would she relinquish her burden.

Her arms closed around him protectively, her fingers stroking the breadth of his powerful shoulders, finding the unexpectedly vulnerable hollow of his nape.

"Stay with me—sleep with me," he urged softly, in no way intimidated by his faltering stamina.

"You need your rest," she said reluctantly. She made an effort to edge toward the side of the bed, and he rolled away, allowing her partial freedom.

"Stay here with me, Belinda." His voice was still husky with emotion, but now it was colored by an unexpected note of humor. "After all that exertion, I'm afraid of a relapse."

Obscurely relieved that she had not been called on to make the decision after all, Belinda entered into the spirit of the game, feeling some of the tension ease away. "All *what* exertion?" She mocked gently. She was amazed at herself, lying there trading pillow talk as if she had done that sort of thing hundreds of times. In spite of all her travels, she wasn't particularly experienced when it came to men. She had certainly never found herself in bed half naked with one before, much less nonchalantly discussing such intimate matters.

"Touché."

Once more she made an effort to escape the heavy arm that held her to his side. "Unless you want to step out of bed into a puddle of shrimp bisque in the morning, you'd better let me go."

"Only if you promise me you'll come back," he parried, the soft rumble of his voice having a decided effect on her nerves.

Oh no, don't start that again, she thought, half in amusement. Aloud, she said, "You'll be starving—after all that exertion. Let me clear this mess away and I'll bring you another bowl of soup. If that one bites the dust, then you're on your own."

"And if I clean my bowl like a good boy, will I get a reward?"

Dodging nimbly out from under the reach of his muscular arm, she giggled. "I'll send Martha up with some pound cake soaked in sherry and cream as soon as you eat your soup."

"That's not precisely what I had in mind," Chandler said dryly. He lunged for her and then fell back, grinning unrepentently as she evaded him. She retied her drawstring, retrieved her shirt and put it on with a singular lack of self-consciousness. Then she set to

work, still laughing, clearing away the debris of the
ruined meal. "I'm just glad I didn't offer you a
four-course dinner."

"By all rights, I should be down there cleaning it
up myself."

"The very idea boggles the mind," she said with
droll horror.

"You think I couldn't?" he challenged.

"Oh, I'm sure you could do anything you put your
mind to, Mr. Harrington, your superiorness, but it's
much more your style to lie back in solitary splendor
while your lowly minions do the dirty work." She
was joking, but when she stood up again, the stained
towel in her hand, she knew instinctively that the
game was over. Seeing the shadow of a frown on
Chandler's face just before he turned away from her,
she sagged visibly. All the exhausting hours of nursing piled onto her shoulders suddenly added up to an
unbearable weight. "I'll be back in a few minutes
with another bowl of soup, Chandler."

Without turning around, he said gruffly, "Don't
bother, thanks. I think I'll sleep awhile."

It was over. Like one of those exquisitely decorated
Easter eggs, she thought, closing the door quietly behind her—so utterly lovely to look at, so incredibly
fragile. She had no idea what had brought about the
brief cease-fire, but whatever it was, she'd never forget the hour of shared lovemaking, shared laughter,
when she had had one tantalizing glimpse of paradise.

The last remnants of that paradise drifted away like
fog under a blazing sun the next morning. Belinda

awakened later than usual, her head thick with the stuffiness that always followed oversleeping. She lay there for several minutes staring at the ceiling and trying to come to terms with the feeling of loss that assailed her.

It had been too much to hope that he'd have forgotten all about seeing her in Cannes, much less that horrendous scene in the library before he'd dashed out. Ironically enough, his subconscious had even supplied French endearments. A fever of 103 degrees might impart a sort of selective amnesia for a little while—a disorientation that could block out something that had happened at the onset—but it couldn't last. Nor did she really want it to. All the same, it had been a delightful interlude—a poignant taste of what might have been if she'd simply come there with no motive other than to look after Steve, never having laid eyes on any member of the Harrington family before, never having agreed to take sides in a custody fight. Starting fresh, there might have been a chance for them.

Except for Enid. She had forgotten Enid. Flinging back the covers, she sat up and swung her feet to the floor, stretching her arms over her head. Her sense of humor rose reluctantly to the occasion, although with an unaccustomed tinge of bitterness. How could any man possibly prefer that scrawny, cold-blooded paragon to a lovely, biddable young country lass like herself? She was no voluptuous beauty, but at least she wouldn't rattle when a man shook her—nor would he have to wear thermal underwear to bed to protect himself from frostbite.

As her body automatically went through her
wake-up ritual in front of the open window, her mind
clung stubbornly to thoughts of Chandler and Enid.
Why couldn't a man who claimed to despise dishonesty see through that conniving witch? Blue blood
couldn't be all that important, even for someone of
his social standing. After all, even royalty had seen
fit, every generation or so, to beef up the stock with
a few sturdy peasant genes.

Steve's room was empty, and Belinda showered
hastily and was tying on a flowered wraparound skirt
when she heard raised voices outside the house. The
window over the portico was open, allowing a fra-
grant breeze to lift the curtains with a gentleness that
was completely at odds with the strident voice downstairs.

"You listen to me, you doddering old fool, I'm
going inside that house, and neither you nor your silly
yard broom is going to stop me!"

It was Enid, and she was livid. With a sinking feeling, Belinda slid her feet into rubber flip-flops and ran
lightly down the stairs to the front door. Poor Duggins
shouldn't have had to put up with that sort of tirade,
but his loyalty was such that until Belinda released
him, he'd stave off an invasion, armed only with gar-
dening tools.

"Good morning, Miss Smathers," Belinda said
calmly, closing the front door behind her. She had no
idea whether or not Chandler was still sleeping, but
she certainly didn't need his appearance on this particular scene.

"What's the meaning of this? I'd like to know!"

The pupils of those cold gray eyes actually seemed to elongate into tiny ellipses. "I know very well Chandler's back home and I demand to see him. And furthermore, you impertinent little nobody, when I get through with you, there won't be a home in the Commonwealth of Virginia that would hire you to scrub the floors!"

"Miss B'linda, should I go get Martha?" Duggins asked anxiously.

"Thanks, Mr. Duggins, but that won't be necessary. Miss Smathers is just leaving."

She interrupted the shocking outburst of profanity that was emerging from Enid's carefully made-up mouth by calmly announcing that Chandler was still under the doctor's care, but as soon as he was allowed visitors, someone would notify her.

"Chandler? Ill? Why wasn't I informed?" If possible, the parchment complexion became even paler.

"He's had some sort of intestinal virus, Miss Smathers. A nasty bug—highly contagious. Steve had it first." Belinda described some of the more unpleasant symptoms with relish, delighting in the look of distaste on the narrow, well-bred face as the visitor actually backed away. Seeing Duggins's tall, thin form disappearing around the corner of the house, Belinda elaborated gleefully. "Of course, if you insist on seeing him, I'm sure he'd be cheered up no end. In fact, seeing that you two are so close, you'll probably want to help with the nursing duties." The need for nursing had largely passed, except for watching to see that the patient didn't overexert, but Enid didn't have to know that.

"Well—actually, I've never been terribly good in the sickroom," the older woman declared hastily. "A private-duty nurse—someone from the hospital. I'll ask Daddy to find someone—he's endowed so many hospitals, I'm sure he can—" She was brushing imaginary germs from her flawless linen suit with a thin, nervous hand, rattling a quarter of a pound of gold bracelets on each wrist.

"That won't be necessary, Miss Smathers. I've been managing pretty well. At least, I've had no complaints from the patient," she added, a wicked smile on her face.

Enid's narrow eyes flashed cold fire. "Enjoy your little fling while you can, my dear. Once Chandler gets rid of his obligations to Bobby's family, one way or another, we certainly won't be needing your services. I'll be hiring a completely new staff, and you can take my word for it, that horrible old man won't be a part of it. He actually threatened me with that—that yard broom!"

Before Belinda could absorb the meaning behind the vindictive words, they were joined by Steve and Thalia. It seemed to Belinda's distracted gaze that the redhead hesitated on seeing Enid, her unusually clear blue eyes clouding over momentarily.

"Hi, Enid. When did you get back?"

Belinda was saved the further embarrassment of exposure by Steve, who piped up to announce that his mother was going to take him out for a real Italian meal.

Enid's scathing glance raked the actress's small but voluptuous figure. "I'd hardly think someone in your line of work can afford to indulge herself in pasta, darling.''

Thalia, seeming more chagrined than insulted, murmured something to the effect that she was between pictures at the moment. ''A girl has to relax sometime,'' she added defensively.

While the child darted off to threaten the perfection of the low boxwood hedge by leaping back and forth over it, Belinda leaned against one of the columns at the top of the wide, shallow steps, numbed as she fought against accepting Enid's remarks at face value. The desultory conversation going on several feet from her flowed around her unheeded, and she was on the point of turning to go inside when a vaguely familiar sedan rounded the curve in the driveway to pull up before the portico.

''Dick!'' Thalia exclaimed. It seemed to Belinda that her smile was almost relieved as she turned to greet the rather diffident man who climbed out from behind the wheel. ''What are you doing here?''

''Hello, Thalia.'' Dick Lovatt's glance took in the three women and the child, who had paused in his hurdle-jumping to gaze at the newcomer. ''This must be Steven.''

With a self-consciousness that was oddly attractive, Thalia made the introductions. Belinda was acutely aware of Enid's needle-sharp curiosity as Dick nodded his slightly balding head—he was only thirty-five, but his thinning dark hair, plus his grave, half-shy manner, made him seem older.

''I know Belinda, of course.'' He turned to offer her a timid smile. ''I was surprised that you stayed on after—uh—well, anyway, Mickey sent along the things you wanted,'' he stammered, turning to retrieve the suitcase from the back seat.

Any faint hope Belinda had harbored of escaping undiscovered fell with a dull thud as Thalia turned a curious look on her. ''Your partner Mickey? But of course! Belinda Massey—Mickey Massey. I guess I just wasn't listening. It didn't occur to me that the girl you sent out here to—I mean—that she was your partner's wife.''

''Sister,'' Belinda muttered softly, but the damage was done.

After casting her a long, speculative look from those disconcertingly penetrating eyes, Enid made her farewells and sauntered past Dick's slightly dusty sedan to her own impeccable Mercedes.

Chapter Eight

Except for the matter of Chandler's disposition, everything was going unbelievably smoothly by the end of the week. Belinda, glancing through the kitchen window to where Steve and Thalia were showing Dick Lovatt the puppies, spoke over her shoulder to Martha.

"Did she say whether or not he's staying for dinner this time?"

"They're going out. All three of them," the housekeeper replied with a significant emphasis. Belinda was well aware of Martha's speculations about Dick's visits. He'd stayed only a few minutes the first time, talking with Thalia out in front of the house after Enid had gone. The next time he had dropped by with some weak excuse about being in the neighborhood. Harrington House *was* the neighborhood, unless he was headed for the Smathers estate, some three miles west.

"Steve seems to like him," Belinda ventured, prying up a square of the chocolate-peanut butter fudge from the shallow pan. "Martha, you're a terrible influence!"

"Don't recall twisting your arm," the older woman retorted dryly. "That Thalia's the one with a sweet tooth. At least it's better than you know what."

Belinda did. There had been no drinking, not even the preprandial sherry, but the actress was spending more and more time in the kitchen as she indulged a newly discovered enthusiasm for cooking rich Italian dishes and baking excessively sweet pastries. Steve was delighted, Belinda amused, and Martha kept her own council. As for Chandler, he scowled at his books, at the mail, at the news, and at anyone who dared enter his presence.

Except for Steve's quick good-night visit—the child alone seemed immune to his uncle's irascible temper—Belinda was the only one with enough nerve to face the surliness that accompanied his recovery. That was because she had nothing to lose.

Belinda took a dinner tray to her sitting room after seeing Dick, Thalia, and Steve off. They were dining early for Steve's sake. She would have enjoyed having Martha's company, but Clarence Duggins had an odd sort of dignity that precluded any undue familiarity on her part.

She returned to the kitchen and arranged Chandler's tray, then carried it up to his bedroom. Since he appeared to be showering, she left it on a table and then hesitated. "You all right?" she called over the sound of the water. He was still a bit unsteady on

his feet, and too stubborn to admit it. His recovery
had been considerably slowed, according to Dr. Timmons, by his almost total exhaustion at the onset. And
earlier that day, in spite of Belinda's threats, he had
insisted on spending several hours in the library. Not
only that, he had informed her that he had to be in
New London, Connecticut, on the following Thursday.

They'd argued about it. Belinda had threatened to
walk out and let him bully the other members of the
household, and he had told her succinctly that she
would leave when he said she could and not before.

"Why don't I just call in Miss Smathers to fetch
and carry for you. I'll bet her bedside manner is something to marvel at!" She had been torn between rage
and fear—the fear that she'd actually walk out and
deprive herself of even the pleasure of his displeasure.

"I'm sure Enid would fetch and carry, as you call
it, as graciously and efficiently as she does everything
else," Chandler had snapped. "At least she's intelligent enough to recognize the importance of my work.
I'll be spending the next few afternoons in the library,
Miss Massey, and I'd appreciate it if you'd refrain
from treating me like a blasted two-year-old!"

But the effort had been too much for him, as evidenced by his gaunt pallor when she and Duggins had
helped him back upstairs. She supposed she should
be thankful he hadn't insisted on going into town.

The sound of the shower ceased abruptly. Belinda
hovered in the doorway, uncertain whether he'd heard
her or not. If he was capable of turning off the
shower, then surely he was all right, she reasoned. All

the same, she was still lingering there when a moment later the door opened and Chandler strode out, his strong, shapely legs bare of all but a covering of dark hair below a short dressing gown.

"You're okay," she muttered, backing out the door hastily.

"You're sure of that," he challenged. The mocking light in his eye did not escape her, nor did it do much for her composure.

"I'll be down the hall. If you need anything, yell out—there's nobody in the kitchen." A bell system ran from the bedrooms, the dining and living rooms, to the kitchen—a holdover from the days of a full staff. Belinda darted out the door and was halfway down the hall when he called her back.

"What is it?" she demanded impatiently. It had been another long day, and as much as she loved him, she had come close to walking off the job several times.

"What happened to the famous Massey bedside manner?"

"This *is* the famous Massey bedside manner! The patient gets precisely what's coming to him—no more, no less."

Her eyes, glinting like sun on deep water, didn't waver as he sat down in the tobacco-brown chair and pulled the table holding his dinner closer. "Tell me about Thalia," he commanded. "She's been staying out of range lately, and you're no mine of information at the best of times. Have the two of you been up to no good?"

"My dinner's getting cold," she told him flatly. As

much as she resented his implication, she refused to be drawn into dangerous waters. The subject of her relationship with Mickey hadn't come up again, but Dick was bound to have told Thalia how she came to be there, and she certainly couldn't trust Enid not to go prying into matters that didn't concern her. She knew she was living on borrowed time, and the feeling wasn't very comfortable; she hardened her resolution to leave as soon as Chandler was solidly on his feet.

"Then bring it here. And that's an order, Belinda."

Not moving from her place in the open door, she bristled. "My working day ended when I brought you your dinner, Mr. Harrington. And now, if you'll—"

"Belinda!" he bellowed. "Dammit, woman, stop dithering! I ordered you to get your tray and join me in here, and if you refuse, I'll go get it myself. Is that what you want? You miss having some lovesick idiot hopping around to do your bidding? Or are you hoping I'll fall flat on my face at your feet, tray and all?"

"Knowing who'd have to clean up after you, it would hardly be worth the pleasure I'd get!"

By the time she returned with her tray he had cleared away the stack of opened mail and untidy newspapers from the table and moved the other chair closer. She emptied her tray and stacked it on his. "All right," she snapped, arming herself with knife and fork. "I'm here, so eat your meal! Tomorrow, you can darned well stay downstairs until dinnertime and let Martha serve you."

He shot her a brilliantly mocking look. "Your solicitude overwhelms me. Tell me something, Belinda, do you dislike me, or are you simply afraid of me?''

"I'm afraid I might strangle you barehanded, if that's what you mean. Heaven help—'' Her lips tightened. She had been about to say "Heaven help your wife if you ever get sick again," but thought better of it. That was a subject she hardly dared broach when she was alone; to discuss it with him would be the ultimate folly!

The pork roast was succulent—crisp and brown on the outside, juicy on the inside—and the fried okra and sweet potatoes in orange shells were out of this world. Thalia had already started putting on a few pounds, to her chagrin. Belinda would have to watch herself or she'd be in the same fix—once she stopped running a daily twelve-hour marathon.

But, of course, in a few days she'd be leaving. From the looks of things, Thalia was on the way to being able to look after Steve. Ironically, the custody fight that seemed to be on hold had been a blessing in that respect at least—and with Chandler leaving for New London the following week, she'd have the perfect excuse to fade out of their lives, her pride, if little else, intact.

If, in return, Chandler didn't oblige her by fading out of her mind, then that was something time would have to cure.

"What are you thinking about?''

She lifted her chin and favored him with her haughtiest look. "I *beg* your pardon?''

He burst out laughing. "Belinda, love, you're priceless! A royal duchess couldn't have done it better.'' His laughter faded, leaving behind a warmth that had been missing for too long, and Belinda applied herself studiously to the crispy cartwheels of fried okra.

"Tell me something, Belinda. What do you think of Thalia's chances of straightening herself out? Is she showing any signs of improvement?"

Caution stilled her hand, and she looked up at him warily. "Do you mean about her drinking?"

"Partly. I guess I should have filled you in on that business before I left for Washington, but I—well, there's already been too much mud slung for one reason or another. Poor Thalia, I can't really blame her, not with a mother like hers behind her and that blood-sucking agent who attached himself to her. I'm beginning to wonder if at least half the trash that's been printed about her wasn't manufactured in his sleazy office." He sliced a thin sliver of succulent meat from the bone with the precision of a surgeon. "It would have been a whole lot easier if she'd been born with a squint and a crooked nose."

"Then you'd hardly have been in a position to worry about her, would you?"

He grimaced slightly. "Probably not—Bobby never bothered with plain women. Or slow cars, for that matter. He'd have been better off if he had settled for something a little less spectacular in both cases."

Belinda removed the plates and poured coffee for them both. "How long has it been?" she asked.

"Since he was killed? A year, almost. Eleven months."

Then Thalia had been widowed for a little over four

months when Chandler had been with her in Cannes, Belinda speculated, hurriedly putting from her mind the unpleasant idea that had been growing there for too long. "Did she drink much before that?"

"Not that I know of—at least, not to excess. But I don't think the drinking has as much to do with Bobby's death as with her own inability to cope with reality."

"Whose brand of reality? Yours or hers."

He stared at his knuckles as he held the cup in both hands. "Fair question—if not a particularly easy one," he mused. "I suppose I've always been a bit hard on her on general principles."

Always? she thought, remembering a certain evening in France. Aloud, she said, "Because she was an actress?"

He shrugged, and Belinda watched in fascination as the dark-blue silk of his dressing gown slithered across his broad shoulders. "You're implying that I'm a snob, and I guess it might look that way on the surface. But, Belinda, it's not Thalia's profession so much as the fact that her background and Bobby's were so completely different. Lord knows, marriage is a gamble in the best of circumstances, but when the partners come from such widely divergent backgrounds, that's doubled in spades. Their goals are totally different, and in most cases, they're not even aware of the fact." He stared morosely into a past that she could only guess at, but her heart felt every bit as bleak as his voice sounded. "Unfortunately, it isn't only the couple who has to suffer for the mistakes."

"Steve," she sighed, and he nodded.

"Thalia couldn't handle her own high-powered world, much less Bobby's. Each of them chose his or her own means of escape. Bobby's was permanent."

Before he could shut the door on it, Belinda caught a glimpse of the hell he must have been through, but when he spoke again his voice was flat, devoid of emotion.

"Thalia had an irresponsible woman along with her this time as a sort of maid-of-all-work. The woman had evidently discovered that by keeping the liquor flowing, her own job was made a lot easier. Unfortunately, Thalia's too easily manipulated, even when she's sober. Drunk, she was a pushover. I got home from a business trip and went by to see Steve and found Thalia totally wiped out, the maid out with her boyfriend, and Steve hungry and scared to death because a couple of nosy reporters had been trying to get inside."

"And you brought him home with you," Belinda said softly. So that's how it had happened. Thalia had probably called her agent in a panic, and he had taken over, milking it for all he could get out of it with the kidnapping angle. Thalia, knowing that Steve was safe with his uncle, had settled for calling Dick, instead of the police, and from then on, the whole muddle had gotten out of hand.

She braced herself to confess her own role in the tragi-comedy, but Chandler went on to discuss his frustration over trying to juggle his work and his personal life, and the moment passed.

"You've told me more than once that I'm no good

as a surrogate parent,'' he pointed out ruefully.
''Maybe it's because I keep on hoping that by some
miracle Thalia will mature enough to take responsibility for the boy herself. Lord knows, I love him—
he's so much like Bobby it tears me up just to look
at him sometimes. But it isn't fair to Steve to deprive
him of his mother when I've nothing to offer him
along those lines.''

Bleakly, Belinda told herself that Enid must have
spelled out the conditions of their future relationship
pretty clearly. Otherwise, he'd have expected her to
tackle step-motherhood with her usual disgusting efficiency.

When Chandler seemed to make a deliberate effort
to shake off his depression, Belinda could only follow
along. After all, she didn't have any answers—at least
none that she dared offer. He held out his cup for
more coffee, and she obliged, pouring herself another
cup as well. *Coward!* If she had good sense, she'd
own up to her embarrassing misdemeanor, wish him
good-night, and get out before he started throwing
things. But then, she'd long since relinquished any
claim to that commodity.

It was insidiously comfortable there in the spacious
bedroom, with the soft glow of lamplight warming
the Wedgewood-blue walls, the muted touches of
ivory and brown. Chandler, for some curious reason,
was in an unusually mellow mood, and as long as she
kept her wits about her, what harm could there be in
prolonging the intimate conversation just a little bit
longer?

As if by mutual consent, they avoided touching on

the immediate problems, and Belinda found herself telling him about some more of her experiences taping folk music in the hills of West Virginia. He countered with several incidents concerning himself and his brother.

"We were convinced we were on the verge of discovering a hidden city in the marshes around Newport News. We spent a whole summer poling our skiff up every little tributary within miles. When we'd run out of water, we had to drag the thing—and that was before the days of fiberglass, remember. We had an old juniper boat that was first cousin to a dugout canoe. Anyhow, we'd drag it through the marsh until we struck water again. It's a wonder we ever found our way out of there."

The talk continued in the same vein, and it was only natural for Belinda to bring up some of the more outlandish experiences of her three summers as an au pair girl. When she mentioned the Cadoux children and an incident that had involved them with Fréjus's gendarmes, it was Chandler who changed the subject abruptly. Whether it was because he didn't want to be reminded of Giles Ebon's effort to involve the police in Thalia's affairs, or because he wasn't ready to tackle the matter they had been discussing when he had gotten sick, she didn't know.

Nothing had changed. In spite of everything that had happened over the previous few days, they were right back where they had started. Her hopes would rise irrepressibly, lifted by the logical assumption that no reasonable man would condemn her on appearances alone—and Chandler, no matter what else he was, was a reasonable man. And then they plunged. Even if he decided she hadn't been quite as wild as she had appeared that night in Cannes, there was the irregularity of her employment. Still, that was a small matter, really—she'd done nothing at all to be ashamed of. Hope began to simmer again, only to be quenched by the cold knowledge that Enid was waiting impatiently in the wings for him to resolve the problem with Thalia and Steve.

As if her thoughts had triggered his own, Chandler said, "Tell me about Thalia's friend Lovatt. I understand he's been showing up on the doorstep every day lately."

The last thing she wanted to do was discuss Dick and his involvement with Thalia. It would be too easy to make a misstep. "They knew each other in high school," she said cautiously.

"So Martha mentioned. What does he do? Do you think they might be serious?"

Skating hurriedly past the first question, she tackled the second. "Dick might be serious—I can't imagine Thalia would be. After all, a woman as beautiful as she is could have most any man she wanted. I can't see her settling for poor old Dick Lovatt, as nice as he is."

"Do you really consider physical beauty so important?"

"No—yes. Oh, I don't know. I thought all men did." She stood up restlessly and gathered the coffee things. Here was another perfect opening to tell him of her connection to Dick and the agency, and she knew she was going to renege again.

Chandler stood up, too, and moved aimlessly around the table to where she was stacking dishes on the tray. Belinda, acutely conscious of his nearness, his warmth, and the clean, masculine scent of his body, heartily wished he had taken the time to put on more than the silk dressing gown.

"Not all men are foolish enough to consider the gift wrappings more important than the gift," he murmured as his hand covered hers, directing it toward the table. "Put down the cups, Belinda, before you break them."

Numb fingers released the bone china saucers, clattering them dangerously against the cups as she braced herself to resist his spell. "I'd better get these stacked in the dishwasher before—before..."

"Before what?" he taunted. He was so close she could see herself reflected in his eyes, and she tried to back away. Her hip struck the table, rattling the dishes, and she jumped as if she had been stung— jumped right into Chandler's waiting arms. His laughter registered on every vertebra in her spinal column, and then his mouth covered hers and the sensation coalesced into a heavy, drugging sweetness that robbed her of all reason.

Hands sifted through her hair, stroked her nape and then moved down over her back, holding her so close that the whole sinewy length of his body was indelibly impressed on hers. Belinda was agonizingly conscious of the single thin garment he wore, of the fact that it had fallen open above the tie belt so that his chest was revealed, its muscular expanse liberally covered with springy dark hair. His mouth was deliberately beguiling her senses. He lifted his face slowly, still holding her around the waist as he leaned away to smile lazily down at her. "We have some unfinished business to attend to."

Belinda was fighting a valiant battle, using what remained of her common sense, and when Chandler began edging her backward toward the bed, she dragged her feet.

"Come now, love. I could always carry you, but you wouldn't want me to overtax myself, would you? Let's conserve my energy for where it will be the most valuable."

"No, wait, I—"

"I've waited long enough, *ma belle*. I've wanted you ever since I first saw you." They were beside the bed now, and Chandler pressed her with relentless gentleness onto the linen spread.

She popped back up again, her wide eyes beseeching. "Chandler, I don't think—"

"You don't have to think, my love. I stopped thinking one night in Cannes when I saw a golden bacchante laughing down from the rim of a fountain at a pair of"—his finger traced the rim of her ear, then curled under her chin to tilt her head so that his mouth hovered over hers—"of silly young men who didn't know how to appreciate what they were being offered." With one knee on the bed beside her, he leaned over and brushed his mouth against hers, teasing, withdrawing, taunting and drawing away again to laugh down at her. But there was no laughter in the warm, dark fire of his eyes when he said, "You can have no conception of how much I envied those boys that night, Belinda. Never in my wildest dreams did I imagine that I'd be given a night of my own.''

Her heart leapt to her throat and lodged there as she hung onto his words, drowning in her need to believe. If she had fallen blindly in love in such an unlikely way, wasn't it just barely possible that he had, too?

He came down beside her, carrying her with him. Bracing himself with an arm on each side of her, he lowered his face to her breast. ''You have on too many clothes again, *Bellefleur*,'' he murmured deeply. ''It seems to me you're always overdressed for the occasion.'' He proceeded to unbutton the front of her pale-pink blouse, laying it open to feast his gaze on the golden creaminess of her body. ''Untie my belt,'' came his dark, velvet command. His whole body was trembling from the fierce control he was exerting over himself. Belinda found it almost impossible to breathe.

Her hands went to the tasseled ends of his sash. Slowly, she pulled on one of them, releasing the knot. Chandler had rolled over onto his side to allow her the freedom, and he reached down to the zipper on the front of her jeans, sliding it with deliberate slowness until it reached the lower limit. His hand slipped into the gap to caress her flat abdomen, one finger sinking into her navel, and she gasped and turned to him blindly.

''Chandler—oh, please, Chandler, you don't know what you're doing to me! I—I can't think.''

''Don't think,'' he whispered hoarsely. ''Feel—just *feel*, Belinda. I promise you, I'll take you every step of the way with me. It will be so good for you, darling—so very good." His words were lost as his mouth came down on her breast, his tongue stroking the nipple into aching erectness. She was dimly aware that her jeans had been removed and had fallen to the floor and the only remaining barrier to his full knowledge of her was a single gossamer garment.

His lips moved slowly down the incline of her small, proud breast to rake across her stomach as his fingers rimmed the elastic of her sheer blue bikinis. Gazing down at the soft lamp glow on his thick, pitch-black hair, Belinda held her breath. She could see the pulsing of her own flesh as her heartbeats drummed frantically. Words of love streamed silently through her head, rose irrepressibly to her tongue, only to be fought down again and again. If only he would tell her! He *must* love her. What else could he have meant? He had remembered her—had wanted her from that first glimpse, just as she had been obsessed with him. It wasn't possible for her to love him so intensely unless the feelings were returned. Fate simply wouldn't allow it.

In the distance, a sound intruded. Chandler's lips had found the hollow at the back of her knee, and his tongue was reaming the dimple there. Her fingers kneaded the elastic muscles of his shoulder convulsively as his kisses trailed upward, and then, at the slamming of the front door, she uttered a startled gasp.

Chandler groaned, his head resting heavily on her thigh for a moment. "I don't even know if I locked the blasted bedroom door," he muttered.

With agonizing slowness, the unbearably high level of passion began to ebb until Belinda was able to think more or less coherently. "That will be Thalia and Steve—and Dick, maybe. She'll be bringing Steve up to get him ready for bed." Her voice was almost unrecognizable—a hoarse parody of itself.

"And he'll want to stop in and say good-night—anything to postpone going to bed," Chandler added, knowing his nephew's penchant for procrastination when it came to bedtime.

Belinda was sitting upright now, and Chandler re-tied his robe and scooped her jeans off the floor. "Where's my shirt?" she murmured, glancing about her distractedly. By all rights she ought to have been numb with embarrassment, but for some curious reason she wasn't. As if such incidents were the most natural thing in the world, Chandler stood up and held her jeans for her to step into, and she braced herself against him as she lifted one foot and stuck it through. He turned his face to kiss her lingeringly on the shoulder just as they heard Steve's tired protests coming closer.

"Hurry," she urged, hopping about on one foot while she managed to tangle the other one in her pants leg. She still hadn't located her shirt, and they were almost up the stairs, with Thalia calling down to tell Dick she'd be back down in a minute.

Belinda spluttered impotently as Chandler pushed her down onto the bed to tug her pants up her legs. "Lie still! If you can't dress yourself, then accept my help with good grace, at least." His voice, still slightly husky from the hastily abandoned lovemaking, held a note of amused indulgence that made her want to pull him down on top of her and let the chips fall where they may.

But the chips were already knocking on his door. "Uncle Chandler, are you awake?" Steve's thready little voice piped.

"Be there in a minute, son. Just let me—" He broke off, laughter lighting his eyes as he caught sight of Belinda's fingers fumbling frantically at the buttons on her shirt almost before she had her arms in the sleeves. "You're doing it up wrong," he whispered, grinning at her over his shoulder as he crossed to open the door a crack.

"O-o-ooh, blast!"

"Hi, son. Did you have a good time? Shall I help you get ready for bed tonight since your mama has a caller?"

The pair of them disappeared, and Belinda breathed a frustrated sigh and started rebuttoning her shirt. The sound of Steve's high-pitched eagerness came to her clearly as she heard him following his uncle down the hallway.

"What's a caller? I had a hamburger and two helpings of French fries and Uncle Dick says if I promise not to fall overboard, he'll take me out fishing in his boat."

Thalia was growing restless; that much was clear to Belinda when she encountered her on her way downstairs the following morning. "I don't know how you manage to look so disgustingly bright-eyed," the redhead snorted. "Your tolerance for boredom must be higher than mine.'' Her eyes held the old familiar hunted look that had been absent for the past several days, since she had taken over Steve's care and indulged in the frenzy of fancy cooking. Evidently, the novelty was beginning to wear off.

"I haven't had time to get bored,'' Belinda replied with a commiserating grin. ''The better my patient gets, the worse he gets, if you know what I mean.''

"I've got to get out of here. I don't mind telling you, a little taste of the hallowed halls goes a long way. Even when Bobby was alive, I couldn't take much of it. There's nothing to *do!* Nobody to *talk* to!'' She sounded amazingly like her son had sounded in some of his earlier tantrums.

"There's Steve,'' Belinda ventured. They had descended to the foyer, and Belinda was suddenly struck by the subtle difference in the room since the first time she had seen it, when she had been knocked flat by a small whirlwind. Even those grim ancestral portraits of Chandler's had a slightly mollified expression for a change. Mostly it was the flowers—large, sprawling bouquets she had collected daily in her walks through the grounds. Until lately she had managed to keep a fresh arrangement in all the main rooms.

Thalia moved off impatiently, and Belinda lingered to sweep up a shower of shattered blossoms from the slightly dusty surface of the table. She wandered into the living room, once chilling in its formality, now comfortably disheveled with newspapers, ashtrays, and a cup and saucer left from the night before. Enid would have had a fit, but Belinda rather like the lived-in air. At least the room looked less like a museum.

She went about absently collecting cups and ash-trays, plumping up the cushions—those on the sofa were noticeably crushed, and she smiled in specula-tion. Could Dick Lovatt have anything to do with Thalia's new restlessness? Maybe she missed having a place of her own to entertain.

Chandler was still sleeping when she had peeked in on him before coming downstairs—a short re-prieve. She wasn't looking forward to facing him again, not after the night before. She was too mindful of the fact that the stronger he grew, the harder it was going to be for her to remain there, especially since Enid would be showing up any day. Belinda won-dered if she could get away with nailing a smallpox quarantine sign to the door, and decided she couldn't.

She made a pot of coffee and darted back upstairs to see if Chandler was ready to order breakfast. He was. He was also ready to declare his intention of having breakfast and dinner downstairs.

"Only if you'll agree to take a nap in the library after lunch," she conceded, arms crossed over her chest as she scowled unconvincingly at him. He looked so darned attractive, even with a dark stubble and his hair on end.

"I will if you'll take one with me," he teased. His face was thinner and paler, but the wickedness of his grin was as effective as ever.

"And just how much rest do you think we'd be likely to get?" she jeered. Oh yes, she could joke about it now, but one of these times she'd run out of luck; both the time and place would be right and Chandler's strength would have returned, and then she'd have to face a decision she had been consciously avoiding.

Oh, great Scott, in this day of liberated women, why couldn't she just walk up to him and ask him his intentions instead of lacerating herself with all these self-doubts? The truth was, in some areas she wasn't all that liberated. It was hard to forget his expressed views on marriage. Compatible backgrounds were all important, he'd said, and while hers was respectable to the point of dullness, it was certainly no match for one of the oldest families in Virginia, one whose fortune already had been established back in the days of clipper ships.

Pushing aside her own problems, Belinda dashed downstairs to see if Martha had started on breakfast yet. Thalia was on the phone, and she flashed a resentful glance as Belinda passed by.

"Well, it seems to me that I might at least have a little privacy when I want to make a personal call," the actress declared petulantly, stalking into the kitchen a few moments later.

"Sorry."

Thalia, her hair brushed haphazardly and her face bare of makeup, began impatiently opening and slamming cabinet doors.

"If you need a cup, they're probably still in the dishwasher," Belinda reached for the door of the machine, and Thalia snapped at her.

"I know where the cups are as well as you do. What I need is a drink!"

Inwardly, Belinda groaned. Calmly, she asked, "So early?"

"Yes, so early!" The normally well-modulated voice rose stridently. "Why not? Is it carved in stone that a person can't have a simple pick-me-up before the stroke of midnight? Oh, you—you *provincial* types make me sick. At least Enid understands. I told her that Chandler's well again, and she's coming over to see him later. I think I'll see if she doesn't want to go out to lunch after that. And you can go back to taking care of Steve, as you were hired to do, for a change."

Belinda was still sitting at the table, her chin resting on her fists, when Martha came in from the rooms she shared with her husband. Why should she feel so despondent just because Thalia was reverting to her old habits? It had been too much to hope that the hausfrau role would last once things returned to normal. Back to the old regimen, with Thalia sulking in her room and Enid being terribly, terribly efficient, and Belinda running herself ragged trying to deal with her feelings for Chandler, keep up with Steve, and save Martha a few steps in the process.

And Chandler—what would he be doing? Working too hard and worrying about his inherited problems while he put his own personal life on hold? The sad thing was that Thalia had actually seemed to be enjoying herself, taking charge of her son and indulging her newfound enthusiasm for cooking all sorts of rich and fattening foods.

It had been too easy, Belinda sighed, pouring herself another cup of coffee and allowing it to grow cold as she stared into space. Problems didn't go away that readily.

"What is it, honey?" the housekeeper asked. She was moving stiffly this morning, her seventy-some-odd years clearly evident.

It wasn't fair to burden Martha. "I think Thalia's getting restless." Belinda sighed in spite of herself.

"It takes her like that. She ought to have married a man strong enough to keep her in line, or saving that, one who'd park her in a little house somewhere and let her raise flowers and young 'uns and move the furniture all around every time she got restless."

Belinda laughed, but one part of her acknowledged that Martha's outdated notions might have something to recommend them in certain instances. "Women aren't satisfied with that sort of thing these days," she said.

"Humph! Women are natural-born nesters—some of 'em aren't going to change just because it's the fashion. That girl ought never to have left her old neighborhood. She don't fit in with that wild bunch—nor with Bobby's crowd either." The sizzle of sausages hitting the cast-iron frying pan filled the room. "He was as bad as she was, but at least he was born to it. That poor girl—picked up out of a walk-up apartment over a grocery store and plopped down in the middle of all that wickedness—no wonder she couldn't settle. Pity she wasn't born plain as homemade sin. Then, like as not, she'd be fat and happy with a good man and a yard full of babies.''

"She did seem to enjoy messing around here in the kitchen,'' Belinda mused as she got down a tray and began arranging it. Slowly, an idea began to form in her mind. She glanced at Martha consideringly, wondering if the housekeeper would be up to it. Of course, they could cater the thing, but that would spoil the whole purpose. First, though, she'd have to clear it with Chandler.

Her chance came when she carried up his breakfast tray.

"You're spoiling me, Belinda.'' He was seated at the table with the morning paper, clean shaven, showered and dressed in dark-gray slacks and a casual shirt.

"If you do all right today, tomorrow you can try coming down for breakfast, too. The only thing still suffering is your disposition.'' She left the tray on a blanket chest and placed his plate of sausage, biscuits, eggs and buttered grits on the littered rosewood table.

"That's only frustration breaking out.'' His grin had all the earmarks of a leer. "Have you had breakfast?'' He seemed unusually relaxed, and Belinda hesitated to erase his smile by bringing up the problem of Thalia.

Still, the matter would be infinitely worse if it continued. And those cozy little luncheons with Enid didn't help matters, either. "Chandler, Thalia's getting edgy. I think she's bored. Could we—do you think we might plan a small party?''

At his swift frown, she rushed on. "Nothing big,

but you see, while you were sick, Thalia took over
Steve and some of the cooking, and she really got
carried away with the domestic bit—her lasagna was
out of this world! I thought if she had something chal-
lenging along those lines, something she could plan
and help with and—''

"Thalia couldn't plan a wiener roast for two,"
Chandler said disparagingly, spreading watermelon
rind preserves on a buttered biscuit. "If you think
something like that would entertain her, call Enid. She
does that sort of thing to perfection."

"I don't *want* to call Enid," Belinda exploded.
"You're missing the whole point!" She shoved her
fingers through the knot she had hurriedly anchored
on top of her head, tilting it a few degrees to the east.
"Look, Thalia's used to having a lot of excitement
going on around her, a lot of people. To go from a
full social life to a—a quiet country estate is—"

"If you mean dull, then say it."

"I don't mean dull! I simply mean—well, maybe
you're underestimating her. That agent of hers obviously hasn't got anything for her, and I think she's
just plain bored. Maybe if she had something to do,
something she enjoyed, it would give her a feeling of
satisfaction, and she just might not need to go prowl-
ing around the kitchen looking for the cooking
sherry!"

"Little Miss Fix-it," Chandler sneered. "A taste of
power really goes to your head, doesn't it?"

Belinda flinched as though he had struck her. "Forget it." She turned to escape before she gave way to

the terrible need to cry, but he was on his feet before she even reached the door.

"Belinda, please. I'm sorry. That was a rotten thing to say, and you know I didn't mean it."

She lifted pain-darkened eyes to his. "Do I? Are you in the habit of saying things you don't mean?"

He reached for her, and she shrank from him. The only indication that he caught her reaction was a slight narrowing of his eyes. "I guess you're right about my disposition, but believe it or not, I've been worried about both of them—Thalia and Steve. I've been thinking about what you said—about my not being much of a substitute parent—and it sort of got to me. You were right, you know." A small muscle flickered in his jaw, and Belinda's eyes clung there so as not to fall into his deep gaze and drown. "I hate to say this, but I'm not very good at admitting to errors in judgment. Quite frankly, I'm not used to making them," he said with disarming candidness. "This fellow—Dick What's-his-name. A small dinner party would be a chance for me to meet him, size him up. Not to mention the fact that I could escape your iron hand long enough to meet with my business partners."

His rueful expression robbed the words of their sting, and she asked, "Do they have wives? That should fill out the numbers just about right."

"Mmhmm. The Shoemakers, the Williames—that would be four—and with the rest of us, that's enough, don't you think? We don't want the cure to be worse than the disease."

Belinda was mentally adding up on her fingers; the two partners, their wives, Chandler, Dick—

"Enid, of course—she's invaluable with this sort of function. Maybe Thalia had better—"

"Yes, perhaps she should," Belinda snapped, hoping Enid was highly susceptible to the miserable virus that was raging through the area.

Chapter Nine

Because of Chandler's trip to New London, Thalia's dinner party was planned for three nights later. That would give her time to tend to all the details of telephone invitations, menu planning, shopping and hiring enough extra help to see that everything ran smoothly. It would also, Belinda observed to Martha, leave little time for growing bored with the project.

"So long as you or Thalia don't come down with that flu thing. Knock on wood," the housekeeper cautioned.

Thalia's first reaction was typically feminine; she had nothing to wear. "All my dressy things are ancient," she declared. "Anyway, they don't really suit me anymore. I think my image has changed—what do you think? Maybe I'll trade in my West Coast glitz for some of Enid's East Coast chic." She examined herself in the mirror, unconsciously tucking in her stomach.

Belinda decided it would be polite to keep her views to herself. She hadn't given a thought as to what she'd wear. It hadn't occurred to her when she came to Norfolk job hunting to bring along a dinner dress.

"As soon as you get Steve settled, Belinda, you can call Soames and have them send out a crew to give this place a thorough going over. Oh, and we'll need somebody to help serve, while you're at it. I may want to hire a chef, depending on the menu I select—I'll let you know later."

A chef! Had she created a monster? Belinda accepted a subtle reminder of her status in the Harrington household with mixed feelings. After all, the purpose of the whole exercise had been to rescue Thalia from the doldrums, not to provide entertainment for the baby-sitter. She'd better not dash out and blow her meager savings on a party dress just yet. She might end up wearing an apron and cap.

The cleaners Soames sent out arrived the following morning. Martha bit her tongue and kept out of the way. She knew the project was therapy for Thalia, and because it mattered so much to Chandler, she was determined to endure it if it killed her. Only later did it occur to Belinda that the elderly housekeeper might actually be enjoying her holiday—probably the first one she had taken since Chandler had moved back into the house.

Thalia spent a whole day shopping for something suitable to wear and came home with a delectable creation in oyster-gray satin. "Darned American boutiques,'' she grumbled, sucking in her stomach. ''Everything's a full size smaller than in France or Italy.''

Which was hardly the case, Belinda thought with amusement as she watched the nicely rounded bottom sway up the stairs with the dress box.

The following day was spent collecting ingredients for the menu Thalia had decreed. Belinda was kept busy running errands, keeping up with Steve, answering Chandler's impatient summonses, and putting the finishing touches on the newly polished rooms. During the morning she engaged Steve's help in gathering everything that was blooming in the backyard, leaving the graceful pink waterfalls of weeping cherry and the brilliant splashes of early flowers to brighten the front yard. Thalia had ordered orchids for a centerpiece for the table, leaving the rest of the arrangements to Belinda.

Steve and Chandler had their lunch in the library, and after carefully hand washing enough of the delicate antique china and crystal, Belinda put together several arrangements for the sideboard and the tables in the living room, with a glowing bowl of tulips, jonquils, and irises for the foyer.

''Everything looks lovely, Belinda,'' Chandler murmured, emerging with both lunch trays from the library. ''In fact, it hasn't looked like this since my mother lived here.''

She was unexpectedly touched. Turning away from the powerfully affecting warmth in his eyes, she placed heavy cut-glass ashtrays around on the occasional tables. ''Is Steve getting droopy yet?''

''Eyelids at half-mast when I left him. He can bunk

down on the sofa while I go through some things I want to discuss with Dennis and Bill tonight.''

"Chandler, you're not to—"

"Slack off, Belinda. I know it gave you a lot of pleasure, having me under your thumb, but I'm back on my feet now. Things are back to normal. You can exercise your Napoleon complex on Steve, hmm?''

Which was more or less what Thalia had told her—that she could go back to doing what she had been hired for. Only as illogical as it was, she resented it when it came from Chandler. "Yes, *sir,* sir!''

"And don't get snippy with me, young lady. I know how to handle you, don't forget." His manner was mild, his voice almost indulgent, but the mocking light that glinted in his eyes left her in no doubt as to his meaning.

Enid had been by twice. Both times, she had walked in on a storm of housecleaning. The first time Chandler had been napping, and Belinda had absolutely forbidden her to wake him. That hadn't won her any popularity contests either.

The second time she had strolled unannounced into the library, where Belinda, Steve and Chandler had been discussing finding homes for the puppies.

Belinda, trying valiantly to push aside her jealousy, had hurried Steve outdoors, where they raced with the puppies until Steve fell in an exhausted heap, the puppies piling on top of him in a flurry of feet, tongues, and frantically waving tails. From the low brick wall where she rested, Belinda watched Chandler emerge to see Enid off. She saw the thin, stylish brunette brush her lips over his before insinuating herself under the steering wheel, and she picked up a twig of sweet shrub and bit down on it hard.

At five-thirty on the evening of the party, Belinda was in her bedroom. The guests were expected at seven, and with Thalia managing the kitchen staff with an iron hand and a fanatical gleam in her eye, Belinda thought it best to keep her distance. She felt a justifiable pride that her idea had been a sound one. Thalia could hardly have poured more energy into the modest affair if it had been an Academy Awards ball.

When the peremptory rap on her door came, Belinda was on her head. Her bare feet were enjoying their freedom after a long day spent racing after Steve and running last-minute errands. She lowered her knees to the floor and righted herself with practiced ease. Her hair was tumbled around her shoulders, her face still flushed when she opened the door to Chandler.

"Hi. Am I needed?" She'd left Steve with Pete, who had finally shown up and had immediately been assigned by Thalia the chore of parking cars—as if the few that would be coming presented a problem. Belinda half expected to see a blaze of klieg lights go on outside the front door.

"There are only eight places at the table. Who's not coming?"

"Nobody's not coming. I mean, everyone will be here, as far as I know."

"Four from my office, the Lovatt fellow, Enid, Thalia, you, and myself. Unless I suffered brain damage from the fever, that makes nine."

"Four couples, Chandler. That's eight guests, or

rather seven and a host. I thought we'd let Thalia sit at the foot of the table instead of Enid, just for tonight. I put Enid on your right and Mrs. Shoemaker on your left, but it's not too late to change if it doesn't suit you.''

"And just where do you plan to sit—in my lap?'' He sounded more irritable than angry. However, when she told him calmly that she'd be busy getting Steve settled and then overseeing the kitchen staff, his brows came down in a ferocious scowl.

"Don't be any more of an idiot than you can help, Belinda,'' he said witheringly. "You'll let Martha take over the boy for tonight and you'll set yourself a place at the table if you have to wedge it in with a crowbar!''

Coming almost instantly to a boil, Belinda strode across the room and threw open the door to her closet. "Fine! And what do you suggest I wear that won't steal the thunder from the little gray satin Falini number Thalia's wearing—this?'' She pulled out her yellow cotton dress. "Or this maybe?'' The paisley skirt. "Or what about my jeans?'' she asked ingenuously. "Jeans go anywhere and everywhere these days, although in all fairness I think I ought to confess, they're not designer jeans. I have an unfortunate aversion to using my posterior as a billboard.''

She had gone too far. As angry as she was, Chandler's towering rage had her backing away from him as he strode across to grab her by the shoulders. "You fractious little—'' He shook her until her teeth actually rattled. "You're a reverse snob, Belinda Massey, and I don't care if you show up in your birthday suit—it's one of the more becoming things you own, as a matter of fact—but be there, you will, if I have to drag you downstairs and strap you into your chair!''

"Chandler, wait!'' she cried as he strode across to the door. ''I need to talk to you about—''

Her anguished eyes stared at the inside of the door that slammed resoundingly after him. ''—something,'' she finished weakly. Her shoulders sagged. She couldn't possibly spend an evening socializing with Thalia, Enid and Dick without waiting constantly for the ax to fall. She'd be miserable. And anyway, she was still only an employee there. Thalia wouldn't expect her to join the guests, any more than she'd expect Martha to, would she?

Dropping onto the love seat, she stared morosely at her bare toes. What had she really expected—that Chandler would suddenly declare his everlasting passion for her and insist that she take her rightful place as his hostess? Fat chance! She might be suitable for a little backstairs hanky-panky, but that was all. Chandler wasn't about to risk making the same mistake his brother had made—not when Eminently Suitable Enid was staking her claim every time she so much as straightened a painting on the wall.

Resignedly, Belinda crossed to her closet to stare at the few garments hanging there. Not much of a choice. She had planned on sending for her books, her musical instruments, and the rest of her clothes from her parents' home once she had a place of her own.

''Belinda?''

He was back again! "What do you want?" she demanded in a surly tone, glaring at the closed door between them.

"Enid will be over in half an hour or so, and she's bringing something for you to wear. I've asked Martha to set another place at the table."

Silence hovered on both sides of the door. Belinda scoured her brain for a legitimate excuse not to go downstairs. Unfortunately, Steve was all settled in with Martha and Mr. Duggins, and Belinda was very much afraid she was sentenced to spending the next few hours watching Enid and Thalia vie for the first place in the hostess stakes.

And if that weren't enough, there was Dick. She'd be squirming the whole time, knowing that at any minute he'd mention something about Mickey, or the agency, or Belinda's part in the whole muddled affair. It wouldn't occur to him that he might be embarrassing both Thalia and Belinda. The soul of kindness, poor Dick wouldn't deliberately embarrass anyone, but he fought a constant battle against shyness, and in his painful attempts to make conversation, he was apt to blurt out almost anything.

Belinda simply *had* to find a minute to talk to Chandler alone. If she could only explain first, she might head off disaster—or at least defuse a potentially explosive situation.

Whether or not it was a deliberate bit of mischief, the dress Enid brought over for Belinda to wear was impossible.

"Sorry, my dear, but this was the best I could do

on short notice. Every rag I own is an original, and there's no room in any of them for your extra poundage, but I think you just might get by with this.''

The ''this'' was an acid-green, heavily beaded caftan. Alone again, Belinda slipped it over her head and stared morosely at her reflection. Enid topped her by several inches, and the thing practically dragged on the floor. She felt like a Victorian lampshade, and to make matters worse, she had nothing to wear with it except a pair of rather utilitarian black kid pumps.

It had been impossible to find a minute to speak to Chandler—first he was showering, then there was a minor crisis in the kitchen, and then Steve couldn't locate the aircraft carrier he usually slept with. Belinda finally gave up. She settled for the rather malicious pleasure of presenting herself to Chandler a few moments before the guests were due.

''Good Lord,'' he drawled in horrified amusement.

''Exactly!''

''Still, I guess it's the best poor Enid could do under the circumstances. You two weren't cut from the same pattern.''

''Oh, I'm sure poor Enid did her best to come up with precisely the right dress,'' Belinda jeered. ''Chandler, do you still insist on embarrassing me this way?''

His eyes moved over her, from the tips of her tailored shoes to the top of her slightly disheveled upsweep, and his voice took on a husky edge when he said, ''I want you there tonight, Belinda.''

Well, he had her there, she thought mutinously a few hours later. The interminable dinner finally over, they had adjourned for coffee. Or perhaps dinner had only seemed interminable to Belinda. She had felt like an extra thumb, wedged in between the two men from Chandler's marine designers firm.

Thalia, after accepting compliments for her shrimp and avocado in aspic, the breast of pheasant on wild rice, and the frozen Drambuie mousse, had spent the entire evening talking in a low undertone to Dick, who seemed more ill at ease than ever in the splendid surroundings. Enid had assumed the role of hostess with practiced ease, directing the conversation away from Belinda all during dinner. As the talk had centered largely on cultural and political affairs in the Tidewater, it hadn't been difficult. Whenever an effort was made to include her in the table talk, Enid managed to field it with consummate ease.

Enid, striking in black peau de soie with an enormous flat bow where her bosom should have been, graciously served coffee in the drawing room, favoring Belinda with a honeyed smile. "The caftan looks lovely on you, my dear. That style is perfect if one has a figure problem. I picked it up at a flea market in London several years ago on a whim, but, of course, I never actually wore it. Luckily, I'd forgotten to throw it out."

Belinda squeezed out a smile that made every muscle in her face ache. "How fortunate for me," she managed through clenched teeth. The partners' wives, Mary and Sara, offered her smiles of commiseration, bolstering her conviction that they cared no more for Enid's brand of polite malice than she did.

After a while Chandler stood and nodded to Bill
and Dennis. They had been talking shop and obviously waiting only for a minimum length of time before disappearing into the library. "If you folks will
excuse us for a few minutes—?"

Into a momentary lull, Enid laughed lightly. "Oh,
must you? I was just going to ask Belinda to tell us
all about her adventures as a lady detective. Surely
that's far more fascinating than your old boats."

"You don't mean it!"

"Are you re-ally? Oh, do tell us all about it!"

Those comments from the other two women. From
Chandler came a level look that revealed neither
shock nor any particular interest. Belinda stared at
him, expecting the ceiling to fall, but when he spoke
it was to suggest that Mr. Lovatt might be a more
authoritative source of information.

Poor Dick flushed a dull red from the sudden attention and stammered something to the effect that it
wasn't at all like the television shows portrayed it.
Thalia, looking around her as if she'd forgotten there
was anyone in the room except Dick, hooked her arm
through his and announced smugly that Dick was only
being modest.

Belinda did her best to become invisible—not an
easy task when one was wearing a concoction of bil-
ious-green silk and multicolored beads.

And then, unexpectedly, she felt released from the
tension that had been growing in her for so long. It
was out now, for better or worse, and she was still
there—although probably not for long. She watched
as Enid stood up abruptly and began moving about

the room with reptilian grace, fingering the rare Faenza bust and a covered vase of white jade that Martha had told her had been brought home by the first Chandler Harrington, a sea captain who later became a shipowner. Enid's muddy gray eyes revealed nothing of her thoughts, but Belinda wasn't fooled. Enid had hoped to embarrass her, at the very least. She must have done her homework well, Belinda thought with bitter amusement. This was to have been the evening when the uppity hired girl was put firmly in her place.

If the dinner itself had seemed unending, the rest of the evening was even worse. The men stayed closeted in the library until after eleven, and Thalia had no interest in anyone except for Dick—which left the other three women and Belinda to get through the time as best they could. Sara and Mary were refreshingly unpretentious, and under any other circumstances Belinda would have enjoyed getting to know them. The conversation, skillfully orchestrated by Enid, however, flowed completely over her head. When the last of the guests was shown out, Belinda could hardly wait to get to her room.

But first she had to check on the state of the kitchen. It would never do for Martha to find it upside down in the morning, and Thalia's interest had fled now that the party was over. She'd lingered outside saying good-night to Dick until Belinda was almost at the top of the stairs, after having found the kitchen in apple-pie order.

"Enid said to tell you good-night," the dreamy-eyed redhead called up to her from the foyer. "Is Chandler still up, or shall I lock the door?"

And bad cess to you, too, Miss Smathers, Belinda sniped silently. Aloud, she said, "He's probably gone up already—may as well lock it."

"This dress is cutting me in half!" Thalia moaned as she shot the dead bolt. "I wish I'd worn something like your caftan. That color looks better on me than it does on you."

"I don't doubt it," Belinda retorted dryly, dragging herself up the last few steps. A stunning redhead could wear most things better than a rather nondescript blonde.

Chandler was waiting in her sitting room for her. She might have known she wouldn't get off scot-free. "Look, Chandler, can it wait until tomorrow?" she implored. "I'm dead!"

"I thought I'd stop in to say good-night. I didn't get to talk to you earlier." In the classic cut of his impeccable evening clothes, he looked dramatically handsome, his lean, saturnine features in no way diminished by the underlying pallor and the pounds he had lost during his bout of flu.

"You should have been in bed two hours ago," she accused, stepping out of the high-heeled shoes and longing to rid herself of the heavy lined-and-beaded caftan. "If you have a relapse now, your trip—" She was talking in circles, deliberately avoiding the subject that was at the forefront of her mind. She simply hadn't the energy to tackle it now.

"Change out of that awful getup and come back,"

he ordered her, dropping wearily down onto the love seat.

"Are you casting aspersions on the efficient Miss Smathers's taste in clothes?" she asked with mock concern.

"Belinda, I'm tired," he said grimly. "Don't push me too far, or you'll suffer for it."

"I've already suffered for it! You forced me to go downstairs and sit through that—"

Chandler, who seldom swore in her presence, uttered an oath that would have tarnished silver. He surged up and reached for her, and before she could escape, he dragged her down so that she was half sprawled across his lap, his fingers biting into her tender flesh. "I warned you," he ground out through rigid lips. When those lips struck hers, they might have been carved from granite. Her mouth was bruised against her teeth, and she struggled, alarmed by the dangerous forces she sensed seething just beneath the urbane surface of the man who held her so ruthlessly.

"Chand—"

"Shut up," he growled against her protesting mouth. His fingers grasped her chin and pulled it down, forcing her to receive the thrust of his invading tongue. He bore her down onto the cushions, and she was dimly aware of the sound of tearing as she felt the thin, musty silk across her shoulders let go.

"Chandler, you're tearing the dress!" she wailed when he released her mouth momentarily to reposition her in his arms.

"Good! I've been wanting to tear it off you all night. To see you sitting there in that abomination—"

"And whose fault is that?" she charged, her anger stoked by his own. What right had *he* to be so angry? It was *she* who had suffered that viper's subtle insults all evening—and some of them hadn't been all that subtle.

Pinning her with the burning intensity of his eyes the same way he had that night in Cannes, he held her in place with one steel-sinewed hand while he caught at the wide neckline of the caftan and ripped the dry-rotted fabric down the front.

She gasped, her eyes darkening in the sudden pallor of her face as her arms went up to cover her bare breasts. "Why did you do that?" she whispered.

But even as she waited for an answer, his eyes glazed over and he caught her to him, the shreds of beaded silk hanging from her shoulders. He buried his face in her throat. "Belinda, Belinda, what am I supposed to do about you? You've been in my blood for so long, burrowing into my consciousness until all I can think of is having you, possessing you—making love to you until I get you out of my system."

Her mind protested even as the old familiar tides began surging through her body. Her last feeble scrap of common sense told her she was a fool for not putting an end to this insanity there and then—and insanity it was.

She made excuses for him; he was tired—he'd been physically and emotionally under stress long before he had succumbed to that debilitating virus. One didn't recover from a combination like that overnight.

And what's your excuse, you spineless fool? That you want him so desperately you're blind to all the dangers, deaf to all reason? Her arms circled his neck and she let her head fall back, offering him the freedom of her throat, her breasts.

One of Chandler's discreet platinum-and-gold cuff links caught in the beadwork, and he swore softly, scattering the tiny glass bugles as he tugged it free. "It's like a blasted spiderweb," he muttered, raking the silken shreds from her shoulders and shifting her to remove it completely.

"Chandler, we can't—I can't—"

His hands were everywhere. His tongue found the small hollows at the base of her throat, and she caught her breath on a shuddering sob. She wanted to tear his clothes off and she hadn't the faintest idea of how to go about it—there were all those studs and cuff links and some sort of suspenders.

"Why couldn't you have worn a—a toga or something," she growled as her fingers reached through the small openings of his starched shirt.

He laughed, and the sound reverberated down to the very base of her spine. "The shoe's on the other foot tonight, hmm?" He lifted one of her bare feet, stroking the sensitive plantar arch until she trembled from the wildly unexpected sensations that coursed through her.

He pushed her aside and stood up. "Not here. Come back to my room, where we won't be disturbed. I don't want any of Steve's nightmares interrupting us tonight." His grin was strained, his eyes burning feverishly, and he pulled her to her feet with unsteady hands.

Grabbing the opportunity offered by the momentary space between them, Belinda said, "Chandler, we have to talk—please." Her eyes implored him to wait, even while her body was clamoring with demands of its own.

"Talk! God, woman, at a time like this? After all the false starts, the stupid blunders, you expect me to sit back, sip tea, and talk?" He swung her against him, pressing his hands against her thinly clad hips. "Does it feel to you as if I'm in any mood to talk?"

Her knees threatened to give way under her as she felt the force of his thrusting masculinity. An avalanche of sensation overwhelmed her, robbing her of her power to think. Nothing mattered, nothing in the world except this man and the irrational physical demands of her own body.

"Touch me," he insisted tensely, guiding her hands on his body. "You need me just as desperately as I need you, Belinda—your body doesn't lie."

Drawing on every vestige of strength at her command, she backed away from his arms, and he let her go, a frown clouding the glitter of his eyes. "Chandler, I have to know…"

"What do you have to know? I should think the most important things between us were self-evident," he said mockingly. Raking a hand through his hair, he muttered, "God! Why is it that women always have to talk everything to death?"

Wounded by his insensitivity, she reached for the jacket he had shed only moments earlier and draped it around her shoulders. It still held his body warmth, and she drew it closely about her as she forced herself to stand her ground. "If that's the way you feel, then I guess there's nothing more to say. I had thought— that is, I'd hoped—"

He shot her a glance that held frustration, anger, and something less easily defined. "All right, you had hoped. So had I, but I'm tired, Belinda, and as much as it goes against the grain to have to admit it, at this moment I have a very limited amount of strength. I have to leave here tomorrow morning—that is, to-day—instead of Thursday. Bill set up an appointment for me in Boston, and from there I'll go on to New London. Meanwhile, Thalia is as apt as not to do something monumentally stupid before I get back, and I had hoped—foolish of me, I suppose—but I had hoped we understood each other well enough so that I didn't have to explain all this to you."

She could have wept. Whatever it was they had had, what little ground she might have gained, was gone now. She had no right even to bring up her own petty concerns, but she simply *had* to say something for the sake of her guilty conscience.

"About the—about my being here under false pretenses," she began, and he cut her off impatiently.

"Are you looking for absolution? Forget it," he said tiredly.

Painfully conscious of how utterly ridiculous she must look, standing in the ruins of that dreadful gown wearing only a pair of beige lace panties and a dinner jacket that swallowed her whole, she struggled for dignity. "I can't forget it, Chandler. It was wrong of me even to—"

"I said, forget it! There's no need for your earnest little confession at this point, so shall we save the baring of the soul until I'm not quite so pushed for time? Enid mentioned yesterday that you were connected with the detective agency, and believe it or not, it didn't overtax my mental faculties to fill in the blanks." His derisive tone made her shudder in embarrassment. "So you came here believing that hoked-up PR release Ebon tried to hand out. It amazes me that any licensed PI could fall for that tripe, but I guess Lovatt couldn't see past those big blue eyes of Thalia's."

Belinda took his scathing contempt at face value. "I can leave the first thing in the morning," she said quietly, drained now of all feeling. "For what it's worth, I'm sorry. I—it seemed like a good idea at the time."

Turning away abruptly, he raked a hand through his hair and then squeezed the tense muscles at the back of his neck. "Oh, honey, look, it's not all that important how you got here. I gather you're related to one of the partners—Lovatt and Massey, right? So it was a natural. And I happen to have pretty solid evidence that your references are legitimate," he added with that odd, self-mocking note she had detected several times of late.

"Then what is it? What's bothering you, Chandler?"

His eyes ranged over her in a leisurely survey. "You have to ask? I should have thought it was pretty obvious. Given a limited amount of time and energy, I'd have preferred not to waste either of them in talking. Unfortunately, you had other ideas. So now, if we've hashed out the matter of your double agentry to your satisfaction, I'll say good-night. The next few days are going to be rough enough without sacrificing a night's sleep."

What could she say to that? He was obviously bored with the whole topic. "Well, if I don't see you again, have a good trip."

"Don't be an idiot," he dismissed coolly. "I'll see you in a few days, and we'll work something out. Maybe by then I'll be able to think straight," adding with a derisive grin, "about nautical matters, at least."

Miserably, she watched him cross to the door. The slate was clear, the demands of her conscience satisfied, and still she felt as confused as ever. It was on the tip of her tongue to ask if he needed help in packing, but she swallowed the words hastily, remembering his response the last time she had dared offer to help him pack.

Chapter Ten

It was later than usual the following morning when Belinda opened her eyes. Her brain felt heavy, as if it were still snarled in the remnants of a disturbing dream. Something had wakened her from her unusually heavy sleep, and she waited in resignation for it to repeat itself.

"Hello-oo. Belinda? You awake?"

"Thalia." She groaned and rolled over on her face. "What's wrong?"

"Nothing's wrong," the redhead bubbled with irritating cheerfulness as she came in to perch on the foot of Belinda's four-poster bed. "Aren't these rooms the pits? Honestly, this stuff is right out of *Gone with the Wind!*"

Belinda struggled upright, blinking at the lemony sunshine that spilled across the floor. She had lain awake for hours, but when she had finally drifted off, she had made up for it with a vengeance. "Has Chandler gone yet?"

"Ages ago. He was stalking around here like a bear with a toothache. I don't envy Enid." Thalia leaned back, bracing herself on her hands, and smiled fatuously at her own reflection in the mirror over the William and Mary chest of drawers. "I don't envy anyone this morning," she added softly.

"Let me guess," Belinda said dryly, ignoring the unwelcome references to Enid Smathers. "Dick?"

With an anxiousness that should have been unbelievable in anyone of her experience, but wasn't, Thalia asked, "What do you think of him, Belinda—honestly?"

Belinda hid the quick stab of envy and slid out of bed, twisting and stretching her body instinctively. "A-ah, ooh—I'm stiff!"

"Well?" the actress prompted impatiently.

Belinda smiled at her, feeling old beyond her years at the sight of all that tremulous expectancy. Counting on her fingers, she said, "I think he's kind, reliable, intelligent—ah, attractive," which was stretching it somewhat, but beauty was in the eye...and all that.

"I think I'm in love," Thalia muttered.

"I believe you."

"I was married before, you know—I mean before Bobby. When I was seventeen. It was over before my eighteenth birthday. I only married to get away from Mama, but it wasn't worth it. I've gone out with scads of gorgeous actors, too, but they're all Peter Pans. Want to know something funny? I even—don't laugh—I even thought I was in love with Chandler once. Can you imagine *me* with any man so cold and worthy?'' A giggle escaped her, and then she added a bit wistfully, ''He is good-looking, though—better even than Bobby was, but Bobby was fun.''

Cold and worthy? Chandler? After a moment of silence, Belinda asked gently if she thought Dick would be fun, and Thalia looked at her indignantly. ''Well, after all, Belinda, at my age there are more important things than having fun, and anyway, Dick likes going to the movies and the beach, and he adores Italian food.''

As her voice rambled on with a list of all they had in common, some of the Southern drawl and a few Virginiaisms crept through the years of drilling in diction. Belinda had ceased to listen. So Chandler had really gone away without seeing her. Was he tactfully offering her a chance to clear out before he returned? He'd mentioned seeing her after he got back and working something out, but she had a very good idea that whatever he worked out would fall far short of her foolish hopes.

''—so we'll probably do it. With Enid and Chandler out of the way until Sunday, there's nobody around to pitch a fit. You know, I'm really glad Chandler got rid of Giles—he was always hassling me. Anyway, I told Dick okay and he's going to call his parents today and—''

''Out of the way?''

Thalia blinked at her. ''Out of whose way? Weren't you even listening?''

''You said, 'With Enid and Chandler out of the way'—I thought Enid was going to be tied up at her father's headquarters until after the primaries. Last night she—''

"Oh, last night," Thalia dismissed. "Enid likes to go on about all that political junk, but I'll bet that even if her father did win an election, she'd think twice about passing up a chance to marry Chandler just so she could go to Washington as a congress-man's hostess."

"So they left together?" She knew the answer as soon as she voiced the question, and a blanket of apathy settled over her.

"Sure, they settled it last night. I thought you knew. Didn't Chandler tell you?"

"Why should he tell me?" Belinda shrugged and reached for her bathrobe. "I think I'll get a shower. Will you see to Steve's breakfast?"

"Okey-dokey. Cold cereal is all he needs, isn't it? You know, he's really a lot of fun now that he's not forever whining about something."

As the door swung closed behind her, Belinda's thoughts shifted briefly to the small boy she had so quickly grown attached to. It was always the same when summer ended and she had to say good-bye to children she had lived with and cared for, nursing them through everything from broken legs to broken hearts, from teething complaints to temper tantrums. But this time, summer wasn't ending. It was spring, the time of rebirth, and she should be looking forward with eagerness instead of looking back with this awful emptiness.

She stripped her bed and put on fresh linens and then emptied all the drawers of her belongings. There was really no point in hanging around. It would be hard to say good-bye to Steve, but he'd be all excited over the trip to Poquoson, where Dick's parents lived. Mr. Lovatt kept honey bees and rabbits, and he and his wife were avid sailors. Steve would adore it.

"You don't mean to tell me you're leaving?" Martha declared later in offended tones.

"Yep." Belinda perched on the edge of the table, nibbling the trimmings of dough from the paper-thin molasses cookies the housekeeper was rolling out. "You know I'm not really needed here anymore, Martha. Thalia can look after Steve now, and she should. And now that Chandler's back on his feet, there's nothing for me to do. Even the house is spotless."

"For a change," the older woman added, slapping another round of dough on the floured, cloth-covered board. "You don't need to spare my feelings, child. I know I'm too old to do, and too cranky to let go, but maybe I will let somebody come in now and again and give the old house a thorough cleaning. My, it does shine, doesn't it?"

"It's lovely. I'll miss it—I'll miss you, too, Martha."

"Pshaw! We both know who you'll be missing, and it's not that boy either. I may be getting past my prime, but there's nothing wrong with my eyes!"

Belinda's reaching hand fell to her lap, empty. There was a certain peculiar satisfaction in having someone else share her secret—like a second opinion on a diagnosis. Only in this case, the prognosis had never been in doubt. She might recover, but she'd carry the scars for the rest of her life.

"I wish I could help you, child. Lord knows, I'd be willing to sit back and let you take over," the housekeeper murmured, arranging diamond and heart shapes on a baking tin, "but with that other one, that Smathers woman, why I may as well pack my bags. She'd not tolerate me for a single minute, nor I her. I've watched her make trouble over every woman she thought Chandler might be halfway interested in— even poor Thalia. Chandler's like most men—a smart woman can make a fool out of the best of 'em." She flounced across to the oven and slid the cookie sheet onto the middle rack, closing the door forcefully. "Well, it looks as if she'll have her way, after all these years, but he's making a mistake. Still, he'll not listen to me. There was a time when he'd come to me with his troubles, but he's a grown man now, not a schoolboy."

"Then it's true? He is going to marry her?" Belinda bit hard on the unpalatable truth, needing to feel the sharp pain.

"Lawsey, Belinda, I can't say for certain sure. A man like Chandler—" Martha rolled out another round of dough and reached for the cutter. "You have to understand, he's been through a lot these past few years. First his father dropping dead like that, and the Missus, his mother, breaking her hip and then, not a month after she came home from the hospital, Bobby had his wreck. She never got over it. Chandler took care of everything, but he had his hands full with his poor mother, and that Thalia never helped matters none—wouldn't stay here—had to go traipsin' all over God's creation. I couldn't look after the Missus and the baby, too, and that Murdock woman is worse than nothing."

She slid the last sheet of cookies into the oven and sank gratefully into a chair, red-faced from the small exertion. "That Enid was here night and day. The Missus couldn't stand her, but she was too much of a lady to let on, so poor Chandler let her take over. He had his offices in Baltimore then, and he was fair wearing himself to a frazzle, running back and forth. Then, the Missus just gave up the ghost—slipped away in her sleep, rest her soul, and him right in the middle of moving his offices to Hampton Roads so as to be near her."

Belinda, her suspiciously bright eyes mirroring the feelings aroused by Martha's story, bit her lip in an effort to still her wobbling chin. She seemed to be reacting like a leaky faucet to everything these days. "When was that?" she asked huskily.

"Let me see, now—that would be nine months come Easter. I'll never see a red tulip that I don't remember..." The thready old voice dwindled off, but before Belinda could escape to her room to indulge herself in a good round of tears, Martha said, "And then that little flibbertigibbet goes trottin' off to France and leaves the boy with that Murdock woman. Chandler wouldn't sit still for that, no siree! He took off after her and brought her back here and read her the riot act, I can tell you! The trouble that girl's caused him."

"I thought maybe—didn't you say...?"

"About her 'n' him? Lawsey, he's got better sense if she hasn't. Like as not, Thalia would marry any man fool enough to have her. She's a clinger. Like that wisteria that's practically taking over the place—pretty as a picture, but it'll strangle the life out of you if you let it. Runs wild all over the place, climbing on anything that stands still."

"Maybe Dick Lovatt…"

"I hope so. Lawsey, I sure hope so."

Belinda slid down off the table, dusting the flour from her fingers. "I'll clean this up, Martha. Then I think I'll try to get away early this afternoon. Thalia and Steve are going to Poquoson with Dick for the weekend. Since Enid's with Chandler, she'll probably come home with him and—"

"And you don't want to be around when they show up."

Belinda nodded numbly, unable to bear the older woman's sympathy.

"Well, we could both be wrong, you know. Chandler stopped confiding in me a long time ago. The more gets piled onto his shoulders, the more he closes up—too much pride, if you ask me. That boy doesn't know how to ask for help."

Belinda took the cookie board to the sink and began to brush off the loose flour. The whole kitchen smelled of spice and molasses. Steve would be delighted.

"I think I'll just let you straighten up a mite in here for me, Belinda, if you can take the time. Some days I feel my age more than others."

Belinda went through the motions automatically,

her mind sorting through the things Martha had just told her. No wonder Chandler looked so tired all the time—no wonder that virus had poleaxed him! In a way, she was sorry she knew about the troubles and sorrows he had been through in the past few years. It would make it all the harder to pry him out of her heart, especially knowing he'd be living there with Enid, who wasn't the sort of woman to bring him much happiness, whether he knew it or not.

She gave the bedrooms a going over and stopped by Martha's room to see if there was anything else she could do before she left.

"If you could just see that the boy has a decent lunch," the older woman ventured. "I hate to ask it of you, but if I can just get my legs up a spell, I'll be right as rain directly. It takes me this way now 'n' again."

Steve was full of what he planned to do over the weekend, and Thalia was full of her own private dreams, if the glow in her china-blue eyes was any indication. For all the appreciation they showed for Belinda's shrimp salad and corn chowder, she might as well have opened up a can of beans.

"Dick's going to pick us up in the morning about eleven," Thalia announced. "He's taking a couple of days off."

"That's nice," Belinda said absently, her mind on her own problems. She took a tray in to the Dugginses, assured Martha that she had everything under control, and then hurried upstairs as soon as the kitchen was in order again.

A slight hitch in her plans—she really couldn't

leave until Martha was on her feet, but that shouldn't be long. Her legs had bothered her before, but she was usually back in action after half a day's rest.

The bed was still piled high with the clothes she had dumped from her drawers, waiting to be packed. She didn't seem to be able to settle down to any one chore long enough to finish it.

On impulse, she dialed Mickey's office. The taped answer came on with Shelvie's seductively voiced instructions, and Belinda hung up thoughtfully. That was odd. Mickey's agency was rather a haphazard operation, but usually there was someone there. Dick might be out winding up his affairs so that he could take the weekend off, but someone should have been in the office.

She dialed the apartment. For all she knew, Mickey might be home with the bug that seemed to have felled most of the Tidewater area—in which case she'd be needed there. "Hello, Mickey?"

"Massey residence, Jones speaking." That husky syrupy drawl, sounding even more drowsy than usual, could belong to only one person.

"Shel, what are you doing there in the middle of the day? Is Mickey sick?"

A brief mumbling in the background, and then her brother came on the line. "Hi, Pretzel, what's up?"

"Mickey, what's wrong? You sound half asleep. Are you sick?"

"Nothing's wrong, and no, I am not sick—and don't ask personal questions, little sister."

"Mick-ey!"

A groan, and then, ''Oh, for Pete's sake, honey, grow up! I'm twenty-eight, not fifteen!''

''You mean you and Shelvie—?''

He laughed at a murmur from nearby, sounding not at all brotherly, and then said into the phone, ''Yes, I mean me and Shelvie. Look, honey, I was glad to let you crash here while you looked for a job, but— well, Shelvie and I had been sort of doubling up before you came, and—well, you know how it is.''

He sounded so apologetic. Belinda was totally crushed. ''You could have told me,'' she said finally in a small voice. ''I'd have understood.''

''Oh, Pretzel, nobody wanted to hurt your feelings. I liked having you here, and besides, Shel needed a break from my slobbism.''

There was more in the same vein, and when Belinda hung up the phone, she simply sat and stared at the instrument. Mickey and Shelvie. Of course. Why else had he sent along someone he claimed had a plate-glass face to do a job that required a certain amount of deception? He knew she wasn't going to fool anyone, Belinda decided with bitter paranoia. He just didn't care, not as long as he had his apartment to himself again. Only she had. As unlikely as it seemed, she'd been able to fit into the Harrington household so easily that half the time she had all but forgotten how she had come to be there in the first place.

So much for brotherly love! At twenty-eight, she supposed love of another sort came first—and maybe it should. If she had to choose between Chandler and Mickey, she knew she wouldn't hesitate. Having to choose would be terrible; having no choice at all was even worse.

The following morning Dick drove off with Thalia and Steve on the front seat beside him, and as Belinda watched them disappear down the driveway, she swallowed a bitter lump of envy. There was an incipient happy ending if she ever saw one. Five years from now Thalia would be fifteen pounds heavier and a hundred percent more relaxed, her face glowing with pride as she forgot all about the talents she lacked and cultivated others that would be appreciated by a proud and growing family.

Martha was hobbling around the kitchen, and Belinda offered to send for Dr. Timmons, but she wouldn't hear of it.

"Times when I forget how old I am, I've got my legs to remind me. These elastic stockings will help, and if it gets too bad, I'll just take to my bed. I can't ask you to stay on, not when you're all set to go."

Belinda had been shamefully easy to persuade. Knowing she'd have to cut her timing to a fine edge, she finished her packing and then spent hours sitting out by the pond or wandering through the lovely, high-ceilinged rooms she had come to love in the few weeks she had been there. The flowers from the dinner party were beginning to wither, and she emptied the vases and refilled them with generous gatherings of everything in bloom. Thalia's rather ostentatious centerpiece was replaced by a simple arrangement of pear blossoms and iris.

She had already stripped her bed and remade it with clean sheets when she thought she'd be leaving immediately, and rather than change it again, she slept on the spare bed in Steve's room as she had the night before. With too little to do except cooking simple meals for three, she drove up to Williamsburg, and on the way back, toured Busch Gardens and Carter's Grove Plantation. When it occurred to her that she couldn't recall a single thing she had seen all day, she gave it up as hopeless and drove back home.

By Saturday night she was ready to lock her bags and take off. Martha was much better, and only the fact that Belinda still had no idea where she was going stopped her. She hadn't the nerve to barge in on Mickey and Shelvie, in spite of their insistence. She just didn't think she could swallow another dose of someone else's happiness.

Chandler and Enid would be home the next day, but certainly not before noon. Meanwhile, she could fix breakfast for Martha and Mr. Duggins, leave something easy for lunch, and still be gone by ten. She was going to have to find herself a cheap hotel until a job turned up, and she'd rather do her looking in broad daylight.

Leaving out the yellow cotton dress and fresh underwear for morning, she closed the latch of her suitcase on the rest of her clothes and carried her white lawn pajamas to the bathroom. From now on she'd simply follow a step-by-step plan—no thinking required. Bathe, shampoo, sleep soundly until seven. Wake up, dress, cook breakfast, set out something for lunch so that Martha could handle things easily enough, and then take off. No looking back.

It had been weeks since she had checked the employment agencies, and she had to make herself think positive thoughts. This time there'd be something for her—something exciting, something that would involve all her energies, both physical and emotional.

Like what? she jeered silently, rubbing her hair ferociously with the thick towel. It was easy enough to plan it all; not so easy to see it through.

She ran downstairs and made herself a mug of hot milk and took a detour through the library for a book. Remembering she had never read the two she had brought upstairs that first week, she plodded back to her room.

An hour later she stood in front of her window and went through the sun-salute routine for the fourth time, and still she was too restless to sleep. Through the open window came a drift of salt air, exotically laced with freshly cut grass, pear blossoms, and the pungent scent of the nearby York River. The mixture was having a decidedly unsettling effect on her mind; it was going to take more than warm milk and positive thinking to put her to sleep that night.

Without conscious thought, she found herself standing in the doorway of Chandler's bedroom. She had remade his bed earlier, allowing her hands to linger and her mind to wander until she had jerked herself up and begun yanking precision hospital corners into the sheets.

Now she crossed to his closet, drawn by a hopeless compulsion, and opened its louvred doors. Except for things like newspapers, business publications and mail, he was an extremely orderly person. A man of Chandler's background—a man who designed ships—would have that sort of mind: a place for everything and everything in its place, first things first....

Her hand moved across the row of flawlessly tailored business suits and came to rest on the olive-drab jacket he had flung on the ground that day for her to sit on. "Oh, why couldn't you have been the sort of ordinary creature who'd have appreciated someone like me? Why do you insist on matching pedigree for pedigree, bank balance for bank balance, and all that unimportant rot?" She breathed in the essence of sandalwood, good woolens, and something that was essentially Chandler, and then closed the door, her chest aching unbearably.

His bed: king-sized, firmly resilient—like the man himself. She had nursed him in this bed, had lain with him there while they made slow, delicious love to each other. She wished more than anything in the world he had been able to possess her completely that night. Lord knows, he possessed her heart and soul, he may as well have her body, too.

On impulse, she turned back the dark-brown spread and touched the place where his head would rest, closing her mind to the head that would rest beside him. Just for tonight, just for a little while...

The room was still dark. There was no way of knowing how long she had been sleeping, nor what had awakened her. Eyes open widely, she lay rigid and waited. She had slept in Steve's room the previous three nights, her own before that, but even so, there was not the slightest confusion when she opened her eyes to the darkness. She knew instinctively where she was—it was as if she could feel him there beside her. The feeling was so real it was uncanny.

Oh no! A cold feeling of dread encompassed her, followed by a hot flood of embarrassment. But the slow, steady breathing beside her didn't change, and gradually her heart resumed its thready beating. He couldn't have known—but how could he *not?*

She argued frantically with herself as she began to ease away from the center of the mattress—which was the size of a small football field. He must have come in dead tired and not bothered to turn on the lights—at least he had been alone! She tried to imagine her feelings if Enid had strolled in with him and discovered her there, and a small groan escaped her lips.

Something clamped onto her wrist, something that felt like warm steel. She froze for an instant, then tugged frantically.

The silence remained unbroken as she was catapulted across the bed to collide with a solid wall of flesh, and then the wall came down on top of her, covering her body, her face, her mouth....

"Chandler, wait! I—stop it!"

"Shut up," he growled, and proceeded to shut her up for an indefinite length of time. When she surfaced again, she took a deep gasp of air and cried, "Chandler, wait, I can explain."

"We'll talk later." His skin was burning through

the thin stuff of her pajamas. Her hands recognized the texture of him; no silk covering his body now. No nothing!

"But you can't—" Her hands against his shoulders somehow lost direction, and instead of pushing, they were curling over his shoulders, sliding slowly over the satiny surface of his back to hold him to her. It was all she could do to breathe with the weight of him pinning her to the bed.

"Belinda, *ma belle*, you don't know—" He broke off to kiss her temples, her eyes, the corner of her mouth. His hands were busy with her clothing. "You can't know what it means to me to find you here, waiting."

"But I wasn't—ah, Chandler." The protest ended on a tremulous sigh as his lips and tongue began a slow, seductive tour of her body. Her pajama top was no longer a barrier.

Her hands slid over the swelling muscles on each side of his spine, then down to the narrows of his waist, and then her fingers were curling into the tautness of his buttocks, pressing him to her.

"Easy, easy, love—I'm on a short enough fuse, as it is," he murmured against her throbbing breast. While his hands efficiently divested her of her remaining garment, his tongue was scouring her small nipple into proud erectness, and she didn't think she could stand it much longer.

"Chandler, I can't—" She couldn't what? Her mind fluttered like a thousand captive doves, and her body shuddered with the force. She couldn't *think* coherently—didn't *want* to think until it was too late.

His hands commenced a slow, unbearably tantalizing journey of discovery, and she ached to make him feel all the things she was feeling. And then her hesitation ended as pure, mindless instinct took over. The taste of his supple skin, the aphrodisiac of his healthy male scent, all of it overcame her inhibitions as he carried her into a world of mindless wonder. He moved over her, and she came to meet him, hesitating only for an instant at the small discomfort, and then all of time constricted into a fiery pinpoint of light and exploded into a tumultuous celebration of life itself.

"And now," he said sometime later, "if you'd care to say a few words, you have the floor." There was laughter under the deep timbre of his voice—laughter and something that rendered her incapable of speech. "What, no words? What happened to all the talking you wanted to do the other times I had you in my arms?"

In a husky whisper against his damp chest, she murmured, "There doesn't seem to be much to say at this point, does there?"

"Oh, that's where you're wrong, *ma belle.* There's plenty that needs to be said, but I believe in first things first."

And what came after first things? She was afraid to ask.

"Why didn't you tell me?" His voice was still rough with emotion. "Precious, I wouldn't have rushed you if I'd known. You—well, how could I know it was your first time? I thought..." He sounded so unsure of himself, she thought wonderingly, almost vulnerable.

And that very vulnerability robbed her of her last defense. "I wasn't sure what you thought, but I knew that you wouldn't have gone through with it if you'd known, and—"

"And?"

She made herself answer truthfully. "And I wanted you to make love to me. Just this once before I go." Her voice wavered off into a whisper, but he heard. He caught her to him, burying his face in her hair.

"Oh, God, my sweetest heart, you're not going anywhere—at least not for a long time, and never without me. Belinda?" Again that strangled note of uncertainty that ripped the very heart from her. "Belinda, am I crazy to hope that you could love me?"

When she would have spoken, he placed a finger over her lips. "Belinda, I can teach you to care. I'm older—I'm not a lot of fun these days, I know, but I could change with your help."

"No!" she blurted, wrapping her arms around his neck. "No, please don't change. Chandler, don't you know? Haven't you guessed? I've been so afraid you'd see how much I loved you and laugh at me."

When he could finally speak again, he lifted his face and studied her quizzically. "Laugh at you? Precious, in case you haven't noticed, I haven't been particularly jovial lately—this past year has been one I'd just as soon forget. The only bright spot was the memory of a pair of green-and-gold eyes I saw for a minute several months ago." He grinned slowly down at her. "I was mad as hell at having to fly halfway around the world after Thalia that night when I saw you. Bobby was gone, and for the sake of the boy, I had to do what I could, but I wasn't in the mood to be distracted by another giddy female, I can tell you!''

She felt a long, muscular leg reach across hers to pin her to the sheet, and she ran her hands down his lean flanks. "Did I distract you? I thought you'd decided I was a fallen woman, luring innocent young boys to their destruction?'' she teased.

"Don't think I didn't want to believe it. I did my best to paint you wicked, for the sake of my peace of mind. I'd succeeded to the point that I didn't recognize you when you showed up here out of context. And still, there was something about you, something that made me want to keep you around until I had time to get to the bottom of it.''

"You wanted to put me on hold," she teased, her hands making a daring expedition on their own initiative.

"I wanted to hold you all right—no argument there," he growled.

"But what about Enid? I got the impression she had a prior claim."

Chandler's lips moved over her eyebrows and came to rest beside her ear. "Then you got the wrong impression. Honey, you have to understand, I was doing my best to juggle four women."

She jerked herself away and stared down at him. "Four!''

"Well, take Thalia. She was all set to make a complete ruin of her life, and all because she'd been pushed into a situation she was temperamentally unsuited for. First the films, the television things, and then Bobby. She thought she had to live up to the public image that agent of hers had manufactured, and it was about to kill her.''

He settled her back down, her head on his shoulder, and they stared up at the ceiling as a new day slowly crept in through the window. ''And then there was Martha. She's going to have to resign herself to taking a back seat sooner or later, but she still thinks I need a nursemaid.''

''Maybe if the back seat is a rocker, and there's a baby or two to rock, it'll make things easier,'' Belinda suggested softly.

''I can see I'm going to have a practical wife.''

''Am I going to be your wife?'' She could barely get the words past the constriction in her throat.

''You already are, for all intents and purposes. We'll start the proceedings today, when and if we make it downstairs, and the rest is clear sailing.''

''You've accounted for two of your four women,'' she prompted, needing to lay to rest the specter of Enid once and for all. Later she could tell him that Martha had already given her a glimpse of what his life must have been like recently.

''Enid,'' he repeated in exasperation. ''It seemed as if every time I came home, she was a part of the furniture. I stubbed my toe on her more times than I care to remember, but how the hell do you tell a lady she's making a pest of herself? She's a capable woman—about as efficient as they come—but somewhere along the line I discovered that too much efficiency can be hazardous to your health. I much prefer a woman who's as apt to be found on her head as her feet—and,'' he added with a wicked inflection, ''from now on, she'll be spending equal time on her back.''

''You mean you're restricting me? Chandler, I may as well tell you, along with books on yoga, there are a few other eastern books I've dipped into.''

His laughter rumbled all through her, setting off hundreds of little secondary tremors. ''You see? I'm already laughing again. Oh, Belinda, you'll never know how much I love you—what a difference you've made in my life. I tried to tell myself you were too young, that I was too old, that you'd never be satisfied with the quiet sort of life I lead. And in spite of all the reasons to the contrary, I couldn't keep my hands off you.''

''I noticed that,'' she observed with mock humility. ''So you've accounted for three of your women. How about number four?''

''Didn't I just finish telling you? There was Thalia, whom I hope will soon be taken off my hands. There's Martha, and you're the only woman I know who could have walked into her house and taken over without instigating a full-scale revolt. As for Enid— Lord help me—I might have ended up marrying her, and that would have been disastrous for both of us. I've never loved her. Sometimes I don't particularly like her, but she's always been available when I needed a partner for some function, and as a rule I was too busy to hunt up someone else.'' His hands were moving in small circles over the flat of her stomach, setting up echoing vibrations deep inside her.

"And then there was you," he murmured, as the circles began to take in more territory. "Did I tell you how generous I was prepared to be about your past lovers? Those gaping young Frenchmen you were drinking with that first time I laid eyes on you?"

"Chandler, they were children of the family I worked for! In fact, we were celebrating Henri's nineteenth birthday."

"Yes, well, that first glimpse might have been misleading, but then there was Mickey."

"My brother?"

"How was I to know that? Fool that I was, I didn't even know what was wrong with me that night I thought you two had had a lovers' quarrel. You told me you loved him, and I was all set to be magnanimous and patch up your differences for you, but I'd probably have scalped the poor guy if I could have laid my hands on him." He had turned onto his side, and one finger was making intricate patterns from her left breast down her body.

"What are you doing?" she trembled.

"Shh. I'm tracing your circulatory system. Now, where was I? Oh—your brother. I was determined to make you forget him until Enid—who incidentally hitched a ride as far as New Jersey with me—mentioned that your brother was a partner in Lovatt's agency. I shed about ten years when it hit me. In fact, when I dropped Enid off at her aunt's place, it was all I could do not to turn around and head for Virginia."

"I was going to leave this morning," she confided softly, her hands launched on a fascinating study of comparative anatomy.

"I'd have found you," he murmured into one of the small hollows of her shoulder. "Fate's already hinted with a pretty heavy hand that we belong together, and I'm not a man to argue against odds like that."

Belinda closed her eyes and gave herself up to the hands of fate.

* * * * *

Do you want...

Dangerously handsome heroes

Evocative, everlasting love stories

Sizzling and tantalizing sensuality

Incredibly sexy miniseries like **MAN OF THE MONTH**

Red-hot romance

Enticing entertainment that can't be beat!

You'll find all of this, and much *more* each and every month in **SILHOUETTE DESIRE**. Don't miss these unforgettable love stories by some of romance's hottest authors. Silhouette Desire—where your fantasies will always come true....

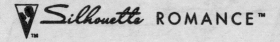
Silhouette ROMANCE™

What's a single dad to do when he needs a wife by next Thursday?

Who's a confirmed bachelor to call when he finds a baby on his doorstep?

How does a plain Jane in love with her gorgeous boss get him to notice her?

From classic love stories to romantic comedies to emotional heart tuggers, **Silhouette Romance** offers six irresistible novels every month by some of your favorite authors! Such as...beloved bestsellers **Diana Palmer, Annette Broadrick, Suzanne Carey, Elizabeth August** and **Marie Ferrarella**, to name just a few—and some sure to become favorites!

Fabulous Fathers...Bundles of Joy...Miniseries... Months of blushing brides and convenient weddings... Holiday celebrations... You'll find all this and much more in **Silhouette Romance**—always emotional, always enjoyable, always about love!

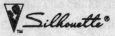